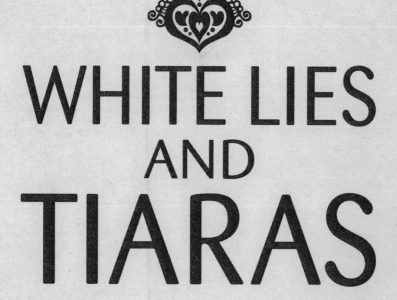

WHITE LIES
AND
TIARAS

ALSO BY MARILYN KAYE

Ticket to Love

MARILYN KAYE

WHITE LIES AND TIARAS

Hodder
Children's
Books

A division of Hachette Children's Books

First published in Great Britain in 2012
by Hodder Children's Books

1

A Catalogue record for this book is available from the British Library

ISBN 978 1 444 90311 9

Typeset in Berkeley by Avon DataSet Ltd,
Bidford-on-Avon, Warwickshire

Printed and bound in Great Britain by
CPI Group (UK) Ltd, Croydon, CR0 4YY

The paper and board used in this paperback by Hodder Children's Books
are natural reyclable products made from wood grown in
sustainable forests. The manufacturing processes conform to the
environmental regulations of the country of origin.

Hodder Children's Books
a division of Hachette Children's Books
338 Euston Road, London NW1 3BH
An Hachette UK company
www.hachette.co.uk

For Isabelle Duquesne-Clerc, and her ongoing efforts
to make me more French

Chapter One

'Miss Henshaw?'

Alice paused at the classroom door and turned back to the professor. 'Sir?'

'Excellent commentary today,' the elderly man declared. 'Your remarks on *Macbeth* were pertinent and insightful.'

Alice stared at him in disbelief. Finally, she was able to choke out, 'Thank you, Professor Grimsby,' before fleeing the room. Nick, who always sat just next to her in class, followed her out.

'Hallelujah,' he said. 'May I offer you my heartfelt congratulations? That was a first.'

'For me, at least,' Alice agreed.

'For anyone! Do you know what he wrote on my last piece of coursework? "This essay is not without some merit." That's his idea of giving praise.'

Her classmate was right – Grimsby was infamous for his total inability to say anything positive to students. Now that the professor's remark was sinking in, Alice could actually feel a never-before-experienced exhilaration.

'I think I'm in shock,' she told Nick as they left the building. 'I can't feel my feet on the ground.'

'This calls for a celebration,' Nick declared. 'How about letting me buy you a coffee? Or even something stronger?'

Alice smiled at her classmate. 'Thanks, Nick, but I've got plans.'

'How about later? Dinner?'

Alice bit her lower lip. She knew she had to let him down, but it wasn't easy. Nick was cute, fit, smart, funny . . .

She spoke gently. 'I can't, Nick. I'm sorry.'

His face fell. 'Boyfriend, huh?'

'Well . . . there is someone I'm seeing.'

Nick sighed. 'Lucky guy. Well, have fun. See you tomorrow.'

He took off, and Alice hoped there wouldn't be any bad feelings. Nick was such a nice guy, and she wouldn't mind hanging out with him sometime . . . but not today. There was another nice guy waiting at the King's Arms, along with her flatmate and *her* nice guy. Even if she wasn't ready to call Callum her boyfriend, she had been seeing him pretty much exclusively. She wasn't sure where their relationship was heading but she had to give it a chance. And that meant not going out with anyone else.

As if to accentuate the unexpected praise she'd just received from the professor, the sky that had been overcast all day responded with an unexpected clearing. It was beautifully warm now and she slipped off her jacket. Then she tugged at the elastic in her hair and released her dark-blonde curls. She wasn't sure why she always felt compelled to wear her hair pulled back when she went to her classes. Probably for the same reason she carried a satchel instead of her favourite fringed handbag. She thought it made her look more serious, more academic. More like someone who belonged at university.

These little tricks were silly, she knew that, but she needed them to bolster her confidence. She'd never expected to find herself at a real university, or even in a real city. Back in secondary school, she'd been a decent student, and she was a great reader, but higher education just hadn't been a dream for her. She'd always assumed that once she left school, she'd take a secretarial course somewhere in the vicinity of Uppingham, the pretty market town where she'd grown up. She'd work for a couple of years. Then she'd marry her childhood sweetheart and raise a family.

But things hadn't worked out the way she'd thought they would. So when her best friend suggested that they both apply to Nottingham University, move to the city and live together, it seemed like a good alternative. So here they were, sharing a flat, going to classes, hitting the library and the student hang-outs, and generally enjoying themselves. And today, for the first time, she realized she was actually succeeding in her studies! Life was good.

She quickened her step. With any luck, someone would have arrived early enough to secure a table in the beer garden. As she walked, she committed the professor's words to memory. She couldn't wait to repeat them to Lara. Her poor roommate had been forced to endure Alice's complaints about Mr Grimsby over and over since the beginning of the term.

Reaching the King's Arms, she hurried through the pub and went directly to the back door that led into the garden. Every table was occupied but then she spotted Harry alone at one of them.

'Hi,' she said, resisting her usual urge to ruffle Harry's

curly hair. There was something very huggable about Lara's boyfriend. Lara herself called him her living teddy bear. 'Where's Lara?'

'Late, as usual,' he told her. 'And your boyfriend's at the bar, collecting drinks.'

There was that word again – boyfriend. Maybe in another month or so, she'd feel differently, but at this point in time she just wasn't comfortable with it. It sounded too much like a commitment she wasn't ready to make. She wasn't even sure if she was looking for a boyfriend. Been there, done that . . . and she wasn't ready to go there and do it again.

The boy who didn't yet have a label was coming towards them now, with a pint in each hand. He was still wearing his work suit, but he'd loosened the tie and opened the top button of the shirt. Still, he looked more mature than most of the guys she knew.

'Didn't you hear me calling in there?' he asked as he plonked the drinks down on the table.

'Sorry,' she said, planting a kiss on his cheek.

'You're forgiven. What do you want to drink?'

'I'll get it,' Alice told him.

He gave her a look of exaggerated horror. 'Do you really think I'd send my girlfriend unprotected into that hive of lonely guys? Now, what are you drinking? Cider?'

'Yes, thanks,' she said, taking a seat. So Callum already felt comfortable calling her 'girlfriend'. This was the first time she'd heard him use the word, and she assessed her reaction. Confusion – that was the only word she could come up with. Callum was a terrific guy, but she hadn't yet felt the bolt of 'I'm-in-love' lightning. Maybe it would come, eventually . . . but hearing him say the word put the pressure on her to reciprocate.

Harry had heard the word too. His bushy eyebrows shot up. 'You're the girlfriend now, huh? When did that happen?'

'None of your business,' Alice replied briskly.

'Of course it's my business; I introduced you two. If you're going out with my best mate, I deserve to know every detail!'

'You're going with *my* best friend,' Alice pointed out. 'Have I ever asked about *your* feelings?'

'You don't have to,' Harry replied. 'You know I'm crazy about her.'

This was true. Harry and Lara had been inseparable for six months. They'd met in a lecture on the very first day of their very first term at Nottingham, and by now Alice was convinced that the concept of love-at-first-sight wasn't a myth. In *her* case, she'd only met Callum a month ago, when he'd moved here to take up a trainee post at a bank. At least she could say there had been an attraction-at-first-sight.

He was a lovely guy, and it was great to have such a nice companion. He was agreeable and reliable; she could count on him. They never argued, they never even disagreed. OK, maybe he wasn't the liveliest of companions but he was always in a pleasant mood, always saying the right thing at the right time and never demanding anything she wasn't ready to give.

'Earth to Alice, come in Alice.'

She blinked. 'Huh?'

'You look like you're on another planet.'

'So would you if you'd just received praise from Professor Grimsby.' She reported what had just transpired. This time, Harry's eyebrows met the curl that Lara was always brushing off his forehead.

'You're kidding! A kind word from His Royal Grimness? That's like the Pope recommending a sainthood!'

'I know, I still can't believe it.'

'You can't believe what?' Callum had returned with her cider.

'The toughest lecturer in the entire English department complimented me on my comments in class.'

'That's wonderful,' he said. 'Congratulations.'

'I'm not sure congratulations are in order yet,' Alice declared. 'Let's see what kind of mark I get at the end of term.'

Harry disagreed. 'You're golden, Alice. You've been anointed. It's smooth sailing for you now that Grimsby's fallen for your charm. Excuse me, your intellect!'

'Uh-oh,' Callum commented. 'Do I have a rival?'

Alice reached over and squeezed his hand. 'Grimsby is about a hundred years old and he bears a remarkable resemblance to a frog. Not to worry, my dear, he's no competition for you.'

'Hi, guys, sorry I'm late.' Slightly breathless, Lara pulled out a chair, plopped down and blew a kiss at Harry.

'Is that all I get?' he complained.

Lara leaned over the table towards him. Putting both hands on his plump cheeks, she tilted his head and laid a big kiss right on his lips.

'There,' she said, releasing him. 'Better?'

'Much,' he said with a grin. 'Alice, tell Lara your news.'

'OK, one more time and that's it! Grimsby said my comments on *Macbeth* were pertinent and insightful.'

'Lucky you!' Lara beamed. 'And lucky me. I won't have to listen to you whine about him any more.'

Callum pretended to be shocked. 'Are you calling my girlfriend a whiner?'

'Obviously you don't know her as well as I do.' Then his use of that certain word hit her. Her eyes widened slightly and she gave Alice a meaningful look.

Alice ignored it. 'How was *your* day?'

'Not bad,' Lara said. 'I got something interesting in the post.' She reached into her handbag and drew out a large white envelope.

'What's that?' Alice asked.

'Not sure, but it's postmarked "France".' She tore it open. 'There are two envelopes inside, one marked for me and one for you.'

Alice opened her envelope, extracted a thick piece of paper and read the embossed words. At first, they didn't register, and she read them again.

'That's nice,' she said at last

'What is it?' Harry demanded to know.

Lara's eyes were wide, and she shot Alice an 'I'm sorry' look before responding. 'An invitation to a wedding. My cousin Jack's getting married.'

'He's the one who lives in Paris, right?' Harry asked.

Lara nodded. 'He's marrying a French girl. At least, I assume she's French. I've never met her.'

Alice looked at the invitation again and checked the

name of the bride-to-be. 'Nathalie, with an "h". And her last name's Dupont. Yes, that sounds pretty French.'

'Wait a minute,' Harry said. 'Isn't he the same age as us, Lara?'

'Two years older.'

'That's still kind of young to be getting married,' Callum commented.

'Exactly what I'm thinking,' Lara replied. 'I'm in shock.'

'What time is it?' Alice asked suddenly.

'Just after six,' Harry said.

She rose. 'I just remembered. I have to pick up my dress from the dry cleaner's and it closes at six thirty.'

Callum immediately pushed his chair back. 'I'll come with you.'

'Don't be silly, you've been at work all day,' Alice said. 'I'll only be a few minutes.' Without meeting Lara's eyes, she grabbed her bag and hurried out of the garden.

Chapter Two

Alice had nothing waiting for her at the dry cleaner's – that had been a rubbish excuse to get away. A million memories had flooded her head and she needed a few minutes alone to collect her thoughts.

There was a small park just across the street from the pub. On this unusually warm spring day, it was full of people, but she managed to find an unoccupied bench. She sat down and let out the breath she felt like she'd been holding since she opened the envelope.

Back at the pub, when she first saw the invitation, she'd managed to show nothing more than some mild surprise and interest. But she knew she had to get away before she lost control and let her real feelings out. Because it hadn't been just a surprise. It was a blow.

Taking the invitation out again, she re-read it.

You are cordially invited to celebrate the marriage of

Mr John Robert Baron to Mademoiselle Nathalie Marie Dupont . . .

'John' was Jack's real first name, but it looked strange and formal to her. The words were embossed on the heavy cream-coloured paper. The date was written out in words, not numbers, and the venue was Château Belleville.

How long had it been since she'd last seen him? At least two years . . . and almost that long since she'd had any communication with him at all. She could remember a time when two days without a conversation would have been inconceivable.

Alice had been eleven years old when she first set eyes on Jack Baron. She could remember the moment as if it was yesterday. It was an August morning, quite warm, and she'd been in the front garden at home, pruning roses with her mother, when the boy on the skateboard appeared out of nowhere. Clearly new to the sport, he was struggling to keep his balance. Then, just at the end of their driveway, he attempted some sort of jump, and toppled into a rose bush.

'Aiiiiiiiii!' he screeched, and Alice and her mother ran over to him.

'Are you all right?' Mum asked anxiously.

Gingerly, he extracted himself from the bush, yelping

12

as the rose thorns pierced his bare arms. That appeared to be his only injury. Once standing, he looked at the damaged bush and his expression was contrite.

'*Excusez-moi, madame! Je suis désolé!*'

'What?' Alice asked. She couldn't understand him.

'He said he was sorry, in French,' Mum answered for him. 'Are you French?'

'Half,' he replied. 'My mother's French, my father's English. I just moved back to England, so I suppose I'm still thinking in French. Anyway, I'm really sorry. I'll pay for the roses. Well, actually, I don't have any money, but my father will pay for them. Do you know Richard Baron? We live on the estate up the road.'

'No, we haven't met yet,' Mum said. 'Alice, why don't you show – what's your name, young man?'

'Jack. Jack Baron.'

'I'm Margaret Henshaw, and this is my daughter, Alice.'

'Pleased to meet you.' He looked again at the rose bush and winced. 'You're probably not so pleased to meet *me*.'

Mum laughed. 'It's not the end of the world, Jack. And I'll forgive any young person with such nice manners. Alice, show Jack where he can clean himself up. Alice! Did you hear me?'

Alice had been staring at the boy in wonderment. And not just because he was new to the neighbourhood. He seemed so different. The boys she knew mumbled and stammered and wouldn't even speak to adults unless they really had to. He *looked* different too. Even in jeans and a T-shirt, with smudges of dirt on his face and hands, there was something about him. At the age of eleven, she probably didn't have a word for it, but looking back now, she guessed it was an aura of sophistication, self-confidence . . . something that set him apart from the kind of boys she knew.

Inside the house, she showed him the bathroom, and then offered him a snack in the kitchen. That was how it began, with crushed roses and a chocolate biscuit. She learned a little about him that day. His parents had divorced when he was six, and his mother had taken him to live with her in Paris. His English father was a schoolteacher, and he'd recently taken a position at the boarding school in town. Jack had been sent back to England to attend the elite institution.

So he wouldn't be going to Alice's ordinary secondary school, but he would be living just down the street. In the weeks to come, that was enough to create a bond between them. At Uppingham School, Jack's classmates were all rich boarders, so the fact that he lived at home with his father and could only afford to go to the school because he got free tuition made him an outsider.

Jack's father was nice, but he was a scholarly person, distant and reserved. His family lived in Uppingham too – a sister, brother-in-law and niece – but he wasn't close to them. He treated Jack kindly, but he just wasn't very communicative. And there were no brothers and sisters. So almost every day after school, Jack headed to Alice's house, where she and her two sisters were always entertaining friends, including Jack's cousin Lara. Jack became one of the gang. To Alice, he was a best friend and confidant – practically a brother.

She couldn't remember exactly when or how everything changed. It just happened. It seemed like one day they were battling over control of a video game, and the next day, they were kissing. And then they were inseparable.

They had their ups and downs, the usual spats and disagreements, but they always recovered from them quickly. As she watched her friends pair off, break up, pair off with someone else, Alice knew her relationship with Jack was special. They were soul mates. It was a connection she couldn't imagine ever having with anyone else.

Then Jack turned eighteen, and to Alice's surprise he

decided he would go to university in France. Alice remembered the long talk with her mother just before he left. Mum had spoken gently, with concern.

'Things will be very different for both of you, Alice. You and Jack have a lovely relationship, but Jack's moving into another world. He'll be meeting new people and having new experiences that you won't share. He'll change, and you'll change too. Hopefully, you'll stay together, but you both need to spread your wings and give each other some freedom.'

Alice didn't argue with her, but she wasn't really listening. She and Jack had spent time apart before. Alice went on holidays with her family, Jack went to France to visit his mother. But they always emailed, called and texted on a daily basis. Distance had never had any impact on their feelings for each other. She and Jack weren't like other couples. What they had was way too special, too unique. Alice knew that in three or four years, Jack would return from university. They would marry, have children, and live happily ever after.

And during Jack's first few months away, everything went just as she imagined it would. He came back to stay with his father in the holidays and spent all his time with her. Then Jack's father left Uppingham to take up a position at another school, way up north, and Jack went to see him on his next break. The calls and emails became less frequent. He was busy, she told herself. Going to lectures, studying and writing essays, nights out with the other students . . . he was too tired to write or call. She tried to be understanding and mature about it, but she missed him terribly.

So she wrote and asked him to stay during the next holiday. She knew they needed to talk, to reconnect, to remember what they had together.

It was over a week before she heard back. That should have been a warning, but she was so naive, or maybe just so stupid, she didn't even fret over it. Maybe if she'd thought about it, she wouldn't have been so shocked by the email he ultimately wrote.

We're too young.

We're not ready to commit.

We need to be free, to have experiences, to meet other people.

We have to be realistic.

We, we, we – when he was really only talking about himself. *She* didn't need freedom, *she* didn't want to meet other people. Suddenly, Jack had decided on his own that all their plans for the future were off.

The shock had been devastating. She'd never cried so much in her life. Finally, the crying stopped and was replaced by anger. How could he do this to her? All that 'too young' business – what nonsense. He'd met another girl and he'd dumped her. That's all there was to it.

She'd found anger was a lot easier to deal with than despair. And Lara had been there for her. *She* was almost as furious as Alice. How could her favourite cousin do this to her best friend? Lara declared that she would never have anything to do with him again.

Lara also tried to help her get over it. She encouraged Alice to go to parties, meet other boys. But Alice, who had never even been on a date with another boy, couldn't think about this. Besides, who would she date? She knew all the boys in Uppingham, and she wasn't the least bit attracted to any of them.

'Come to university with me,' Lara had suggested. 'There'll be lots of single blokes there.'

So Alice did, and Lara had been right. There were lots of guys, and Alice went out with them. The sadness and the anger faded, and she was able to put Jack to the back of her mind. She honestly believed he was dead to her.

But now he'd returned from the grave, and the old feelings came back with him. And why had she received an invitation anyway? If he'd wanted to make it very, very clear that he'd moved on with his life, he couldn't have thought of a better way.

Alice re-read the invitation. Nathalie, with an 'h'. Was this the girl he'd dumped her for?

She shivered, and realized that the sun was beginning to set. How long had she been sitting here? The others would be getting worried. Quickly, she stuffed the invitation back in her bag, got up, and walked rapidly back to the pub.

With the drop in the temperature, her friends had moved inside, and she found them studying the menu board.

'Sorry to take so long,' she said as she sat down. 'I ran into someone and we started talking.' She turned to the menu board. 'What looks good?'

'Where's the dress?' Callum asked.

Alice looked at him blankly. 'Huh?'

'You went to pick up your dress from the dry cleaner's, didn't you?'

'Oh, right! They closed early, I'll have to go back tomorrow. Mm, chicken-and-mushroom pie, that's for me. What are you guys having?'

She smiled at the approaching waitress. But even as she placed her order in what sounded to her like a normal tone of voice, she could feel Lara's wondering and worried eyes on her.

Chapter Three

Lara tried to be discreet, but she couldn't take her eyes off Alice. She knew the business about the dry cleaner's had been an excuse to escape. Alice was putting on a good show, smiling and chatting. But Lara could see straight through her. The invitation had had a much bigger impact than Lara would have anticipated. She could have kicked herself for presenting it to Alice here, in front of the boys. If she'd known what the envelope held, she would have waited until they were home.

Still, she was a little surprised by Alice's reaction. Yes, Jack had broken Alice's heart, but that was two years ago. Alice never talked about him, and it wasn't like she didn't have a boyfriend now. Still, Jack wasn't just another 'ex' for Alice. While Lara could count at least half-a-dozen guys who'd held the title of boyfriend, she knew Jack had been Alice's one-and-only.

She was distracted by the arrival of their food. The waitress placed steaming pastry-crusted bowls in front of each of them. The chicken-and-mushroom pies smelled wonderful.

Harry's pie smelled good too but she knew what it contained and she wrinkled her nose. 'How can you eat that?'

Harry plunged his fork into the pie and took a long look at what he extracted from it. 'You know, if this little hunk of deliciousness was called something other than a kidney, more people would appreciate it.'

'You just dripped gravy down your front,' she pointed out. Dipping her napkin in her glass of water, she made an attempt to wipe it off. 'I despair! That is definitely going to stain.'

Harry wasn't concerned. 'Fine by me. I'll have a souvenir of an excellent pie.'

Lara sighed. How could she love this boy?

Harry addressed the group. 'You know, when Lara and I were having a cuddle once, she left a lipstick print on my white shirt. It wouldn't come out in the wash.' He grinned. 'Think I cared?'

Lara smiled. *That* was why she loved him. 'Aren't I lucky?' she said, rolling her eyes.

'You certainly are,' Alice replied cheerfully. A little too cheerfully, Lara thought.

Callum looked at Alice. 'Aren't you going to say how lucky you are?'

Alice reached over and prodded him in the ribs. 'How's your pie?'

Interesting, Lara thought. Earlier that evening, Callum had referred to Alice as his girlfriend. Now he was giving her the opportunity to put him in the same category. Alice didn't seem to be ready for that and Lara couldn't help wondering if the wedding invitation had something to do with this.

The evening broke up early because Harry had an exam the next day. 'Early bed for me,' he declared as they prepared to leave.

'You go on,' Callum told him. 'I'll walk the girls home.'

'Why?' Harry asked. 'It's only five minutes away. They don't need an escort.'

'He's being a gentleman,' Lara informed him. 'You could learn something from him.' This was something else she loved about her boyfriend – she could tease him, and he could take it.

Harry brushed that off. 'He's not a gentleman. He just wants an excuse to get into the flat.'

'You *are* a gentleman,' Alice told Callum. 'But Lara and

I are fine walking alone. I could do with an early night myself, and you told me you've got a meeting first thing at the bank.'

It took her a while to convince Callum, but eventually they went their separate ways.

'OK,' Lara said as soon as they were out of earshot. 'Start talking.'

'About what?' Alice asked innocently.

'Well, for starters, you can tell me how you feel about Jack getting married.'

'It was a shock,' Alice admitted.

'You're really upset?' It was more of a statement than a question.

'Lara, we split up two years ago. It's ancient history. But seeing that invitation, well . . . it just stirred up some old feelings.'

'I'm so sorry,' Lara said. 'If I'd know what it was, I wouldn't have given it to you at the table.'

'I know you didn't mean to. Can we talk about something else, please?'

'OK. How about the fact that Callum called you his girlfriend tonight? That's the first time I've heard him say that.'

Alice nodded. 'Yeah.'

'So? How do you feel about *that*?'

Alice spoke slowly. 'Good. I think.'

'So is he your boyfriend now?'

'I don't know!' she said finally. 'I *like* him. A lot. What's not to like? He's cute, he's fun to be around, but . . .' She hesitated.

Lara finished for her. 'But you're not in love with him.'

'Not yet,' Alice admitted.

'You've been seeing him for almost two months,' Lara said crossly. 'If you don't know how you feel by now—'

'Wait a minute,' Alice interrupted, laughing. 'Not everyone falls in love at first sight, you know. You were just lucky.'

Lara had to agree. 'It's funny, isn't it? Remember when I used to tell you about the man of my dreams? Tall, devastatingly handsome, elegant, rich . . . and I end up going out with a short, chubby student who dresses terribly and could definitely do with a lesson in table manners. Plus he tells Dad-jokes.'

'He's also head over heels in love with you,' Alice noted.

Lara grinned. 'He is, isn't he? And he always makes me feel so, so—'

'Happy?' Alice offered.

'Yes. And comfortable. He fits me, you know? Like shoes you've had for a long time.'

Alice burst out laughing. 'What a compliment. Harry will be thrilled to know you're comparing him to your trainers.'

'I love my trainers too,' Lara said. She decided it was time to get back to the original subject. 'Alice . . . I know you loved Jack, but—'

'Lara!'

'You did!' Lara persisted. 'Didn't you feel it when you first met him?'

'That was ages ago! And we were just kids.'

'Fine, so are you going to the wedding?' They'd reached their building, and as they climbed the three flights to their flat, she added, 'The invitation included a plus one.'

'A what?'

'We can bring dates, it's on the RSVP card. What do you think? Should we invite the boys?'

Alice paused in the middle of turning the key in the lock to their door. 'Are you crazy? *I'm* not going!' She opened the door. 'And before you ask, *no*, it's not because I couldn't bear to watch Jack get married – it's because I can't afford it!'

'But April in Paris! It would be fun.' She paused to hit a button on the iPod deck.

'There's the transport, first of all,' Alice pointed out.

'And I'm sure Paris hotels are not cheap. I'm going to put the kettle on. Do you want a tea?'

'Yes, but, Alice, I have to go to this wedding – he's my cousin, even if he is an idiot for what he did to you. Please come with me. I'm going to be so bored without you.'

'You won't be bored; you'll have Harry with you. I don't even understand why I got an invitation,' Alice called out from the kitchen. 'I mean, it's not like Jack and I are still friends. We haven't spoken for two years.'

'Maybe it's one of those huge weddings where the couple invite everybody they've ever known,' Lara suggested.

With the music and the whistling kettle, Alice didn't hear her. Lara considered the situation. *She* wanted to go. She'd never been to Paris, and she was pretty sure she'd be able to talk Harry into accompanying her. But it would take the pressure off Harry if he had friends to talk to when all her relatives would be there. She needed to convince Alice to come too, and bring Callum.

Lara went down the corridor to her bedroom. There, she got down on her hands and knees and searched under the bed. Finding what she wanted, she brought it back to the sitting room.

Alice put the two cups of tea on the coffee table. 'What's that?' she asked.

'My photo album. I just got the urge to look at some old pictures.' She flopped down on the sofa next to Alice and opened the book. 'Look, remember that Christmas? When we gave each other the same handbags?'

'I've still got mine,' Alice said.

'And look, remember that picnic? We'd just laid out the food when it started to rain.' She turned a page. 'My sixteenth birthday party. There's you and Jack, over in the corner. That must have been right before he left for France.'

'Mm,' Alice murmured.

The phone rang.

'I'll get it!' Alice said, clearly desperate to get away from the trip down memory lane. 'Hello? Oh, hi, how are you? Yes, she's here. I'll just get her.' She beckoned to Lara. 'It's your mum.'

Lara took the phone and headed down the corridor so she could hear. 'Hi, Mum. I bet I know what this is about. Did you get the invitation to Jack's wedding today? I was pretty surprised.'

'That's putting it mildly,' her mother replied. 'Do you know anything about this?'

'Not a clue,' Lara said. 'I haven't heard from Jack in

ages. Did you talk to Uncle Richard?'

'Yes, he says Jack sent him an email about it a couple of weeks ago. Typically, my dear brother didn't bother to inform me. He said he forgot.'

Recalling the habits of Jack's absent-minded father, Lara laughed. 'And not just to call you. He probably forgot that Jack's getting married.'

'Quite possibly,' her mother agreed. 'He also told me that his ex-wife called him. She wanted the names and addresses of Jack's friends from secondary school. The only one he could remember was Alice's.'

'Yeah, she got her invitation today too.'

'Poor Alice! Well, I certainly hope *you're* planning to go. That's what I'm ringing to talk to you about. Your father and I won't be there because we're going on a cruise – we made the reservations almost a year ago.'

'Oops.'

'So will you go? Represent the family?'

'I'm not sure. It'll cost a lot.'

'Well, we could help you out. Richard told me there are very inexpensive rooms at the château. And if you make your Eurostar reservations a month in advance, you should get a good price. I'd like to think there will be someone from the family other than Richard to sit on Jack's side in the church.'

'It's not in a church, Mum, it's in a château.'

'Well, you know what I mean. It's very strange, isn't it? People usually send wedding invitations months in advance. And Jack's not even twenty-one.'

'It's pretty sudden,' Lara agreed. A thought occurred to her. 'Do you think Nathalie's pregnant?'

'Lara!' her mother answered primly. 'We'll have less of that. Now, what are you going to wear?'

Anxious to get back to Alice, Lara informed her mother that she had absolutely no idea and ended the conversation. Back in the living room, she noted that Alice was still looking at the photo album. In fact, she was still looking at the photo of herself with Jack. That was not a good sign.

'Alice?' she said gently.

Alice slammed the album shut. 'What?'

Lara knew her friend's expressions and she could identify this one easily. She sat down beside her.

'You're still angry at him, aren't you?'

Alice shook her head. 'I don't know. Maybe I'm just remembering how I felt *then*.'

Lara remembered too. 'You were utterly shattered.'

Alice didn't deny it.

'Which is a good reason to go to the wedding,' Lara declared.

Alice stared at her as if she'd lost her mind. 'Why? If just looking at the invitation brings back bad feelings, why would I want to watch him get married?'

'For closure,' Lara said simply.

Alice rolled her eyes. 'You sound like an agony aunt. Or one of those radio psychologists.'

'But I mean it,' Lara insisted. 'You'll be able to close the book on the whole business. Plus, you'll show him you're not still pining for him.'

'And how will I do that?' Alice enquired.

'By bringing Callum. OK, I know you're not ready to call him "boyfriend" yet, but Jack won't know that. He'll see that you've moved on . . . You have moved on, haven't you?'

She watched Alice's expression carefully. Was that uncertainty she was seeing? She pressed on.

'And you haven't just moved on with your love life. You're at university, you're going to be a journalist – you're a completely different person!'

Still no response.

'And you can't tell me you're not curious about this girl he's marrying. Mum says the whole marriage thing seems very sudden to her. I'll bet she's pregnant, but Mum went mad when I suggested that.'

Finally, Alice spoke. 'It's still so expensive . . .'

'Not according to my mother,' Lara said, and repeated what she'd been told about the Eurostar fares and the rooms at the château. 'Plus, Mum said she'd help out with the cost, and I'll split that with you.'

Alice bit her lower lip, and Lara was optimistic. This was something Alice always did when she was having a mental debate.

Just then, Alice's mobile rang.

'Hello? Hi, Cal. Yes, we're safely home. OK, I'll see you tomorrow. Bye. No, Cal, wait.' She looked at Lara, and Lara nodded vigorously.

'Cal . . . do you want to come to that wedding in Paris with me?'

Chapter Four

Alice had been to London before, but it was the first time she'd seen St Pancras Station. The terminal looked more like a shopping centre than a station, with all the cafés and nice shops. She paused in front of one to look at some shoes displayed in the window. Lara joined her there, and Alice pointed out the shoes.

'Wouldn't those be perfect with my blue dress?'

'The one you're wearing to the wedding?'

Alice nodded. 'Slingbacks are sooo sexy.'

Lara shook her head. 'I think your beige ones are nicer.'

'Mm . . . maybe. I'm not sure.'

'Why are you so worried about shoes?' Lara asked.

'Because I want to look good,' Alice said.

'For Callum or for Jack?'

'For *myself*!' Alice declared.

'But I'll bet you wouldn't mind if Jack sees you looking fabulous and has just a little twinge of regret,' Lara said impishly.

Alice grinned. 'It would serve him right for what he did to me. Not that I really expect to get much attention from him. Remember when we went to Chloe's sister's wedding in Devon last summer? There must have been a gazillion guests. We couldn't get near the bride or groom.'

'True,' Lara agreed. 'But we'll just have to find a moment where you can plant yourself directly in his line of vision.'

Alice struck a pose and affected a seductive voice. 'Check it out, Jack. See what you gave up.' She caught a glimpse of herself in the window's reflection, and she couldn't help feeling rather pleased with herself. She *had* changed a lot over the past couple of years. Her hair was longer, and the blonde streaks gave her a sophisticated look. The remnants of adolescent acne that had plagued her when she was seventeen were gone now.

It wasn't just the hair and skin that had improved her general appearance. Being at university had given her more confidence, more self-esteem. And she knew it showed. Yes, she was definitely ready to face her ex and lay the past to rest. And maybe then she'd be ready to move forward with Callum.

'Are you nervous?' Lara asked suddenly.

'About seeing Jack?'

Lara nodded. 'What if it turns out you still love him?'

'Lara!'

'Well, it's a possibility, isn't it?'

Alice considered this. It was true; her reaction when she'd first learned the news of Jack's marriage had been pretty strong. It was definitely possible that somewhere in the back of her mind there had been an insane notion that someday they'd reunite. But that was weeks ago.

'It won't happen,' she told Lara. 'But I know this. If there are any feelings still lurking in a corner of my heart, this wedding will drive them out.'

Lara nodded, and Alice knew she understood. Alice was traditional enough to believe that marriage was a true, life-long commitment. If she saw Jack joined legally in matrimony, she'd be able to rid herself of any lingering doubts.

Now it was time to stick her ex back in the corner of her mind and concentrate on the current man in her life.

'Where are the guys?' she asked Lara.

'Picking up sandwiches at Pret. We're meeting them there.' Dragging their suitcases behind them, they strolled through the terminal. 'You know, I'm hoping it will have a major impact on Harry.'

'What, Pret?'

'No, stupid – Paris! It's the most romantic city in the world. Harry is *not* the most romantic man in the world. And we're staying in a castle!' She smiled dreamily. 'I'm imagining a moonlit night, a room in a turret, candles, soft music . . .'

The boys were just emerging from Pret when they arrived, and both were carrying large paper bags.

'Good grief!' Alice exclaimed. 'It's only a two-and-a-half-hour journey. How much did you buy?'

Callum grinned. 'This was Harry's idea.'

Harry elaborated. 'We need to stock up on good British food before we're trapped in the land of frogs.' He opened his bag to let the girls peer inside. 'Cheese and pickle sandwiches, salt and vinegar crisps . . .'

'I kept telling him, French cuisine is the best in the world,' Callum told the girls. 'He just starts fantasizing about English breakfasts.'

'Hey, I know what the French eat,' Harry declared. 'Pigs' feet, brains, intestines – all the animal parts we throw out.' With an exaggerated shudder, he added, '*Snails!*'

'You're the one who eats kidneys,' Lara protested. 'Anyway, I like snails.'

'No, you like garlic and butter,' Harry said. 'You put enough of that on shoe leather and it'll taste good.'

'I'm in love with a peasant,' Lara sighed.

'And what about foie gras?' Harry continued.

'What about it?' said Lara.

'Do you know how it's made?' Harry asked. 'Farmers stick pipes down the throats of geese and ducks. Then, two or three times a day, they cram pounds of grain and fat into their stomachs. Their livers grow to about ten times the normal size.'

'Harry, you're making me feel sick,' Alice murmured.

'Ignore him,' Callum said. 'He's just showing off.'

But Harry wasn't finished. 'It's animal cruelty, force-feeding them like that. It's torture! And it's against the law in Britain. I'm telling you, guys, we're going to an uncivilized country.'

Callum slung an arm round Harry. 'Don't worry. I'll protect you from the ducks. *And* the geese.'

'Yeah, and what about the French?' Harry demanded to know. 'How are you going to protect me from *them*?'

Callum laughed. 'I won't. I'll use you as a human shield.'

Seconds later, Harry had him in a headlock. A couple of passers-by looked at them in alarm and quickened their pace.

Lara and Alice exchanged looks. *Boys*.

Alice glanced up at the departures board. 'Come on, it's time to check in.'

It was like being in an airport. They had to show their passports, put their bags on a conveyer belt and walk through a metal detector. They had just enough time to change some pounds into euros before going through one more ticket-and-passport check. Then it was down a long, steep escalator to board the sleek, high-speed train.

Leaving their suitcases on the racks by the train entrance, they made their way down the aisle to their reserved places, two pairs of facing seats. Moments later, the train began to move.

'*Au revoir*, civilized world,' Harry said.

'Wow, you speak *French*?' Alice mocked him.

'*Au revoir*,' Harry repeated. '*Bonjour. Merci.* Erm . . .'

'I did two years of French in secondary school,' Lara said. 'Although I'm not sure I can remember much.'

'I just remembered something else I know in French,' Harry announced. '*Voulez-vous coucher avec moi ce soir*.'

Lara gave him a look. 'And if I hear you saying that this weekend, you're a dead man.'

'Even if I say it to you?' Harry asked with a mischievous grin.

Lara batted him over the head with her magazine.

The comment got Alice thinking. What *were* the sleeping arrangements for the weekend? Lara had taken care of all that, and it hadn't even occurred to Alice to ask about them.

She posed the question carefully. 'How many rooms are we going to have at the château?'

'Not a clue,' Lara said. 'My shaky French wasn't up to booking so I asked Jack to sort it out. Is anyone else hungry?' She opened the trays that were between their facing seats, and put the Pret bags on them.

As the others began exploring the contents and picking sandwiches, Alice considered the possibilities. If there were two double rooms . . . how would they separate? Lara and Harry had been together for quite a while now, and Alice knew they were sleeping together. But with Callum . . . She didn't know if she was ready to take that step. What was he expecting? He was such a gentleman; he would never pressurize her into anything. He might have hopes though. And she couldn't blame him. They'd been seeing each other exclusively for almost two months now.

She needed to get Lara on her own to ask if she could share with her. But Lara was so looking forward to this romantic weekend with Harry that Alice felt a bit mean. How could she expect Lara to give up being alone with Harry?

And maybe once Alice had seen Jack, she just might be ready to seal her relationship with Callum.

'King prawn cocktail or mature cheddar and pickle?' Harry asked her.

At least this was an easy decision. 'Cheddar, thanks.'

Lara was leafing through the Eurostar magazine she'd found in the seat pocket. 'I still can't believe we're really going to Paris,' she murmured happily. 'To a wedding in a castle!' She turned to Harry. 'How romantic is that?' she asked hopefully.

Harry put an arm round her. With the other hand, he took a huge bite of his sandwich.

'The castle isn't actually *in* Paris, is it?' Callum asked.

'Just outside,' Lara told him. 'I checked on the Internet, and it's only thirty minutes by train. So we'll have time to do some sightseeing.'

'I know it's corny,' Alice remarked, 'but I really want to go to the Louvre and see the *Mona Lisa*.'

'Look at this,' Lara said. She turned the magazine round so Callum and Alice could see a photo. A young couple, arm in arm, walked along the Seine river at night. In the background, the Eiffel Tower was lit up, and the couple seemed to be bathed in a golden light.

'That's what *I* want to do,' Callum whispered in Alice's ear.

She took his hand and squeezed it. How lucky she was, to be going to Paris with a guy who could appreciate the romance of it all. Forget the past, forget Jack . . . this was now. And suddenly she felt much better about everything. It didn't even bother her when Lara brought Jack back into the conversation.

'I'm still surprised they're having the wedding in a castle. It sounds so aristocratic. Jack was never like that.'

'Maybe he's changed,' Callum suggested. 'You haven't seen him in a long time.'

'It's usually the bride who makes all the wedding decisions,' Lara noted. 'I expect that's why.'

Harry ripped open another bag of crisps and passed them around. 'Do you know anything about her?' he asked.

'No one's met her yet, not even Jack's father. I'm picturing someone terribly elegant, very chic. Hey, I think we're going into the Chunnel!'

Alice shivered.

'One hundred and fifty feet under the seabed,' Harry commented.

'Shut up, Harry,' Alice muttered.

'I think I just saw a fish,' he added.

40

Callum must have sensed her nerves. He put up the armrest that separated their seats and put his arm round her. She rested her head against his chest. It felt so good . . . and she made herself a promise. At some point over the weekend, if she kept feeling the way she felt right now, she would use the word 'boyfriend'.

After only twenty minutes in the Chunnel, they emerged in France, and a short time later the train pulled into Gare du Nord.

'North Station,' Lara translated excitedly. 'See, I *do* remember my French!' But then an announcement in rapid French came over the system. Alice looked at Lara with a knowing smile.

'Did you understand *that*?'

Lara's face fell. 'Well . . . not *all* of it.'

It was followed by the same voice speaking in English, telling them what they already knew – that they'd arrived in Paris, and to make sure they collected everything they'd brought on the train.

They gathered their stuff and joined the queue to leave the train. Picking up their suitcases, they stepped down on to the platform and followed the crowd to the exit.

'Does anyone know how we get to the château from here?' Callum asked.

'We don't need to,' Lara replied. 'Jack's picking us up.'

Alice looked at her in surprise. This was news to her. She let the boys move ahead and pulled Lara aside.

'Why didn't you tell me?' she whispered.

Lara replied promptly. 'Because I knew you'd get all hot and bothered, and you'd be fretting all the way here.'

Alice glared at her. She'd assumed she would have time to shower and change before seeing him. Which was only natural. People always wanted to look their best before meeting someone they hadn't seen in a long time. Especially when they were hoping to make that someone regret the past . . .

They were walking rapidly, and dragging their suitcases, so she didn't even have the opportunity to pull out the little mirror in her handbag. As they approached the end of the platform, she could see a crowd of people waiting for arrivals. She took Callum's hand – for support? Affection? Or simply to demonstrate to Jack that she too had moved on? Oh, *why* couldn't she make up her mind as to how she felt?

She spotted Jack immediately.

However he may have changed, it wasn't physically. Maybe his hair was a little longer. Quickly, she reminded herself of how nice it felt to run her fingers through *Callum*'s silky blond hair.

Jack saw them and started waving. Lara reached him first and they embraced. Then he turned towards Alice. She didn't open her arms for a hug – instead, with a smile firmly planted on her face, she leaned forward and performed a brief air kiss on each of his cheeks.

'Isn't that how the French do it?' she asked brightly. And before he could react, she said, 'Jack, this is Callum.'

Lara introduced Harry, and the boys shook hands. Then Jack turned to his left. 'Everyone, this is Nathalie.'

Alice hadn't even noticed the girl standing alongside Jack. '*Allo*,' she chirped, and kissed each of them on both cheeks.

'*Bonjour*, Nathalie,' Lara said.

Nathalie's eyebrows went up. 'Ah, you speak French,' she said in heavily accented English. And she continued to speak rapidly in her native language.

Lara interrupted her with a feeble smile. 'Um, I'm sorry, I didn't understand that. My French is a little, uh, rusty.'

Jack translated, clearly embarrassed. 'Erm . . . She wants to know if . . . ah . . . you're my childhood sweetheart.'

'No, that's me,' Alice said.

Nathalie turned and fixed huge blue eyes on her. 'Ah, your boyfriend, he marries. Is OK for you?'

'Yes, it's perfectly OK for me.'

Nathalie's gaze dropped to where Alice and Callum's hands were clasped. She looked relieved.

Jack smiled, and Alice smiled back at him. Yes, this was how it was supposed to be, she thought. Childhood sweethearts, that's all they were.

Only her heart was pounding, and a sudden chill engulfed her. She was tired, that was all, she told herself. Tired and a little anxious. It was totally normal.

But she clutched Callum's hand tightly as they followed Jack out of the station.

Chapter Five

The tinny, recorded voice spoke first in French and then in English. 'On your right, you will see Notre-Dame Cathedral, one of the finest examples of French Gothic architecture. Construction on the cathedral began in the twelfth century . . .'

As the voice droned on, Alice clutched the boat railing, and leaned out as far as she dared.

This had been Jack's idea, to take a boat cruise down the Seine before heading out to the château.

'I'm surprised Jack suggested this,' said Callum coming up behind her. 'It seems to me that if you're getting married in two days, you'd have better things to do.'

Alice agreed. 'I know. I couldn't believe they even had time to pick us up. I hope he doesn't feel obliged to entertain us while we're here.'

'He seems like a nice guy,' Callum said.

'Yeah, he is,' she said lightly, keeping her eyes on the passing view. Despite what Lara had said, she really wasn't using Callum to make Jack jealous. She liked being with Callum, she wanted to be with him. But she had to admit that bringing a boy who clearly adored her was going to make her feel a lot more comfortable around Jack.

It was lovely to watch Paris go by. It was almost like watching a film. She had to keep reminding herself that this was the real thing.

She looked back over her shoulder at the rows of seats where most of the tourists were gathered. Harry was flipping through a guidebook. Lara was huddled with Jack, probably bringing him up to date on family news.

Alice hadn't spoken to Jack at all since greeting him at the station. With the whole group together and everyone talking at once, there hadn't been any opportunity. Maybe that was for the best. That shudder she'd felt when she first saw him – was that the anger coming out? If so, she hoped that would be the end of it. She had absolutely no intention of having it out with Jack, demanding to know why he'd dumped her two years ago. She wanted closure without confrontation. Her hope was that the bad feelings would fade away and she could get on with her life. With Callum standing right by her side . . .

'Hey, Cal, check this out,' Harry called, and Callum went over to look at whatever Harry had found fascinating in his guidebook. Alice's gaze moved to Nathalie, sitting on Jack's other side. She looked bored, and it wasn't hard to guess why. News of people you didn't know couldn't be very interesting, even if they were about to become your family by marriage.

This was her first chance to make a good, long, unobtrusive appraisal of the girl. She looked very French, there was no question about that. She was petite – Alice decided she couldn't be bigger than a size six. If what Lara had suggested was true – that she might be pregnant – there was certainly no evidence of it. Her shiny, dark-brown hair was cut in a perfect bob that just grazed her shoulders and her eyes were huge and blue.

She was dressed simply, with no flash or drama, and everything looked right. Her jeans were slim-fitting, but not skin-tight. She wore leopard-print ballerinas on her feet and a plain white T-shirt peeked out from under a fitted black blazer. Of course, she wore a scarf. Maybe it was a cliché, but Alice was under the impression that French girls wore scarves all the time. Nathalie's was a small red and black print. The one item that screamed expensive was the bag hanging over her shoulder. It was immediately identifiable, with the famous LV initials that covered the brown leather.

She realized then that Nathalie was staring right back at *her*. Quickly, she dropped her gaze but it was too late. Nathalie had started towards her, and suddenly Alice was acutely aware of her own outfit, the clothes she'd chosen for travel comfort – leggings that were now wrinkled, a baggy, shapeless sweater, trainers. She managed a smile as the girl joined her at the railing.

'You look at me?' Nathalie asked. She almost sounded as if she was accusing Alice of something.

Embarrassed, Alice didn't want her to think she was being evaluated. 'Oh! I was, um, admiring your handbag.'

Nathalie stroked the bag. 'Is nice, yes? It was *cadeau* . . .' Her forehead puckered. 'How you say in English? Gift? From boyfriend.'

Alice was surprised. Jack used to hate labels – he couldn't understand why people wasted money on designer duds. She couldn't imagine him spending a small fortune on a handbag.

'Not Jack,' Nathalie added quickly. 'Other boyfriend. From before Jack.'

'Ex-boyfriend,' Alice said.

Nathalie nodded. 'Yes, ex-boyfriend. Like Jack for you. You had gifts from Jack?'

Alice tried to remember. She and Jack had never had much money. For birthdays they gave each other music, books, little trinkets. She vaguely recalled a key chain that had broken almost immediately. There was one thing she still had – a huge cuddly bear that he'd won at a fairground.

She didn't want Nathalie to think that Jack was some kind of cheapskate. 'Yes, there were gifts.' To reassure her, she added, 'But it was a long time ago. A very long time ago.' She changed the subject. 'How did you and Jack meet?'

'We meet at a *fête*. End of year.'

'A New Year's Eve party?'

'*Oui*. So now we are together three months.'

'You mean years,' Alice said.

'No.' She counted on her fingers. 'January, February, March. Now is April.'

Alice couldn't help feeling a little shocked. 'You've only known each other three months?'

Nathalie nodded. 'It was, how you say . . . love at first seeing.'

'At first sight,' Alice murmured.

'Six weeks after, he give me this.' Nathalie held up her left hand.

Funny, Alice hadn't even noticed the ring. It was pretty small – a tiny diamond on a thin gold band. 'Very nice,' she said.

Nathalie brushed off the compliment with a wave of her hand. 'It comes from mother of Jack. Is old ring. He promise me, some day he buy me new ring.' A slight smile flickered. 'Already, I choose one.'

Lara and Harry joined them. 'What are you guys talking about?' Lara asked.

'The engagement ring Jack gave Nathalie,' Alice told them. 'I think it was the ring Jack's father gave his mother.'

Lara grinned. 'So she didn't mind giving it away.'

Fortunately, Nathalie didn't seem to have understood that, but Alice continued quickly anyway. 'Nathalie was just telling me that she and Jack met last New Year's Eve, and it was love at first sight.'

'Join the club!' Harry declared in delight. 'Just like "the Larry".'

Nathalie was clearly puzzled. 'What is "Larry"?'

Lara rolled her eyes. 'It's a little game he plays, combining the names of a couple to show how they're joined as one. Lara plus Harry makes "Larry".'

Harry explained further. 'I call Cal and Alice "the Calice". You and Jack would be "the Jathalie".' He frowned. 'It doesn't roll off the tongue, does it? I've got it! You guys can be "the Nack".'

Nathalie was understandably puzzled. 'But your real name . . . it is Harry, yes? Like the English prince.'

'Exactly,' Harry said. He took on a serious expression and affected an exaggerated upper-class accent. 'An old family name, doncha know.'

'Yes, Harry has a title,' Lara added. 'The Duke of Dorkdom.'

Now poor Nathalie looked totally confused, but she did a good job of acting interested. 'The duke of . . . what?'

Alice was distracted by a passing sight – a large square, dominated by a column that had to be eighty feet high surrounded by fountains. 'Is that an important place, Nathalie?'

She glanced at the monument with a dismissive attitude. 'It is not special.'

The recorded guide voice disagreed. 'We are now passing the Place de la Concorde. During the French Revolution, this was the site of the infamous guillotine. King Louis XVI, Queen Marie Antoinette and many others were executed here.'

Alice looked at Nathalie, who didn't react. Clearly history wasn't her thing.

'Do they sell anything to eat on this boat?' Harry asked.

'You ate three sandwiches on the train!' Lara exclaimed.

Nathalie wasn't as critical. 'I think maybe there is food to buy, below. Come.' She linked her arm through Harry's.

Callum appeared. 'Where are they going?'

'To get something to eat,' Alice told him. 'I think there's a snack bar downstairs.'

'I wouldn't mind a Coke,' Callum said. 'Do you want anything?'

Alice shook her head. 'No, thanks.'

'I'd like something to drink,' Lara said. 'I'll go with you.'

Alice was perfectly content to remain where she was alone, and she was rewarded with her first real look at the Eiffel Tower. In her mind, it was the symbol of Paris, and even though she knew it was a touristy thing, she hoped there'd be time over the weekend when she could go to the top of it.

'Nice, huh?'

Jack had appeared at her side.

Alice smiled briefly. 'Yes. Very nice.'

'At night it's really beautiful. It's all lit up, and every hour the lights are golden. I've seen it a million times but it still gives me a thrill. It's almost dusk now; the lights should be going on pretty soon.'

Alice nodded. 'You like Paris.'

'Who wouldn't? It's never really felt like home though.'

There was a silence, and Alice had to come up with something to fill it. 'Nathalie seems nice. Very Parisian.'

He smiled. 'Yeah, but she's not. She grew up in a village in the south of France. She came up here to go to university.'

'Oh.' There was another silence. Alice shivered.

'Are you cold?' Jack asked.

'No, not at all.' She really wasn't. It had been the same kind of shudder she'd experienced when she saw Jack at the train station. Actually, it was more like a mild electric shock, and that was alarming, because she knew what it meant. She didn't have to search her memory to remember the times she'd felt it before, and who she'd been with.

Stop it, stop it right this minute, she told herself. *Stay angry. Just don't let it show.*

'How's your family?' she asked politely.

'Pretty well. Father's arriving on Saturday. Mother's here, of course. She remarried, you know.'

53

'No, I didn't know that.'

'She's now Madame Jean-Louis de Trouville.' He made a face.

'You don't like him?'

'He's a real snob, makes a big deal about being an aristocrat.' He grinned. 'You know, people are always joking about how the British are class conscious. But let me tell you, the French are worse. If they have a "de" in their surname, it signifies some kind of noble lineage, and they're very proud of it. It's much more prestigious to have the right name than a lot of money.'

'And your mother's husband is like that?'

'Mm. Except he's got money too.'

Alice had never met Jack's mother but she remembered the stories he used to tell about her, how she hated being an English teacher's wife, how she wanted to find a man back in France who would give her a grander lifestyle.

'Sounds like Mummy finally got what she wanted,' she commented.

'Exactly.'

They shared a knowing smile, and then she stiffened. They'd made a connection – and this was exactly what she wanted to avoid. She was relieved to see Callum approach with a Coke in each hand.

'I know you said you didn't want anything but I thought you might have changed your mind,' he said.

She laughed. 'You just don't want me drinking half of yours.' She accepted the Coke. 'Look, Cal, there's the Eiffel Tower.'

'Beautiful,' Callum said. He turned to Jack. 'You like living here?'

'Yes,' Jack said. 'I miss England though. Once I graduate, we're going to move back.' He looked around. 'Where's Nathalie?'

'She's downstairs with Harry and Lara,' Callum told him.

'That Coke looks good, I think I'll get one myself,' Jack said.

After he left, Callum moved closer to Alice. 'I didn't realize you and Jack had been a couple.'

'I suppose I should have mentioned it. But it's been over for more than two years.'

'Really? And you're still friends?' Callum shook his head. 'I have no desire to see my ex again.'

They'd never spoken about their pasts before, and Alice looked at him with interest.

'When did you break up?'

'A year ago. She wanted us to move in together and I wasn't ready for that.'

Alice nodded vigorously. 'We're all just too young to settle down.'

'Jack doesn't seem to think so,' Callum noted.

Alice changed the subject. 'Do you still think about her? Your ex?'

'Not since I met you.'

That was nice, really nice. She moved closer to him and took his hand.

A cry of delight rose up. The lights of the Eiffel Tower had come on.

'So beautiful!' Alice gasped.

'I'd like to see the view from the top while we're here,' Callum said.

And then another sight caught her eye. Along the banks of the Seine, a young couple walked, hand in hand. Suddenly they stopped and went into a tight embrace. Even from this distance, Alice could sense the passion between them. She tightened her grip on Callum's hand and nodded in their direction.

'I'd like to do *that* too,' she whispered.

'Right here and now? In front of all these people?' Callum pretended to be shocked. 'We're British, Alice!'

She looked up at him. 'But we're in France.'

She was always comfortable in his arms. And he was such a good kisser. She wasn't sure if she could create more passion than what she'd just witnessed on the banks of the Seine, though she made every possible effort to match it. She didn't shiver or shudder . . . but who needed electric shocks? Maybe it was enough just to feel good.

Chapter Six

Crammed against the door in the front seat of Jack's car, Lara stuck her head out of the window and strained to get the first glimpse of the château. As they rounded a bend on the tree-lined road, it rose up before her and she gasped.

'It's a castle!'

At the wheel, Jack laughed. 'That's what château means in English, Lara.'

'I *know* that. I just didn't think it would be so – so—'

Nathalie provided the word in French. '*Magnifique, n'est pas?*'

'Totally,' Lara agreed.

The ornate white stone building had three levels, with turrets and towers, and it looked like a picture from a fairy tale. There was a huge fountain in front and the entrance was an arch with elaborate carvings around it.

'Is like your château, yes?' Nathalie asked. 'In England.'

'*My* château?'

'She means Buckingham Palace,' Jack said.

'Yes, where lives your Queen.' She turned to face the passengers in the back seat. 'You go there?'

'All the time,' Harry said. 'Dinners, balls, private audiences with Her Majesty . . .'

Nathalie's huge eyes got even bigger. Surely she couldn't be taking him seriously, Lara thought. But just in case, she said, 'He's having you on, Nathalie.'

Clearly Nathalie didn't understand the expression, so Lara put it another way.

'He's making it up.' But Nathalie's face remained blank, and Lara gave up. To Harry, she said, 'I'll bet you've never even been on a tour of the palace.'

'Who needs a tour?' he replied airily. 'I know every inch of it. Wait a minute, we're in France. I meant to say "every centimetre".'

It wasn't that funny, but there was something about the way Harry could say silly things that always made her smile.

Jack parked the car and they all got out and went around to the back to get the bags out of the boot. Lara took her suitcase, but her eyes were still on the château.

'What's the deal, Jack?' she asked. 'Did you win the lottery?'

'It isn't expensive to rent a place like this for a weekend – châteaux are two a penny in France. The aristocrats can't afford to actually live in them so they hire them out for events. It was cheaper to rent this château for the wedding than have it at a hotel in Paris.'

'It can't be *that* cheap,' Lara said. 'Are you working?'

'Just doing a law internship. Mother's paying for the wedding. Actually, I guess I should say Jean-Louis is paying.'

'Oh, to have a rich stepfather.'

Jack made a little face. 'I have a hard time thinking of him that way. We don't really have much of a relationship. I didn't want him paying for this but Mother insisted.'

'But you're not following in your mother's footsteps, are you?' Lara asked as they walked towards the entrance.

'Hm?'

She looked over her shoulder to make sure Nathalie wasn't in hearing distance. 'You're not marrying for money?'

He was clearly aghast. 'Lara! Who do you think you're talking to?'

'Oops, sorry about that,' Lara apologized. 'Just because

you've been around your mother doesn't mean you've turned into her.'

'No. Anyway, not that it's any of your business, but Nathalie's an orphan. She works in the university canteen just to pay her tuition fees.'

Lara looked back at the pretty bride-to-be with new respect. Appearances could be deceiving – Nathalie certainly didn't look like a poor orphan.

'She doesn't know much English, does she?'

'I'd say her English is about on the same level as your French,' Jack said with a grin. The others joined them, and Jack took Lara's suitcase. The boys and Alice went into the château and Lara looked around for Nathalie. She spotted her sitting on a bench near the fountain.

As she approached, she saw Nathalie reach into her handbag and pull out a pack of cigarettes. She was about to light one when she saw Lara.

Indicating the cigarette, she said, 'You will not tell?'

'Tell who? Jack?'

She nodded.

Lara considered giving a lecture on the dangers of smoking but Nathalie probably wouldn't understand it. 'I won't say anything.' She couldn't resist adding, 'Of course, you know it's not good for you.' She didn't add, 'especially not in your condition,' because she still didn't know if the girl was pregnant. But she couldn't resist looking speculatively at Nathalie's midsection.

The girl pursed her lips briefly into something like a pout. At the same time, she tilted her head and raised her eyebrows slightly. It was a funny little movement – it seemed to say 'I don't know' and 'I don't care' at the same time. It reminded Lara of the way some people said 'whatever' – as if whatever they were responding to had very little importance.

'So . . . smoking is your guilty secret?' she asked, with a smile so it wouldn't sound like she was criticizing her.

Nathalie did another little pout. 'Man and woman . . . there are always secrets.'

Lara wasn't so sure about that. There were things about her life that Harry didn't know, but she wouldn't call them secrets, just subjects that had never come up. Was there anything she wouldn't want Harry to know? OK, maybe the fact that she had her upper lip waxed occasionally.

'What are you studying at university?' Lara asked her.

She didn't get the pouting lips this time, but she got Nathalie's other standard reaction – the blank look that demonstrated her lack of comprehension. Lara tried again and spoke very slowly.

'What do you study?'

'At university?'

Didn't I just say that, Lara thought, but she didn't voice it. 'Yes, at university.'

Nathalie took a long drag on her cigarette. 'Books.'

Lara took this to mean that she studied literature. 'Alice is reading literature too. English, of course. I assume *you're* reading French literature.' When Nathalie nodded, Lara searched her mind for something to say about French literature.

'*Les Misérables*,' she exclaimed, remembering that she'd seen the show last year. She could always fake having read the book. 'I just loved it. I felt so sorry for Jean Valjean; he just couldn't get a break, you know? It's a French classic, isn't it?'

'*Oui.*'

Lara struggled to remember the author's name. It had been on the programme, but she couldn't come up with it. 'Who wrote it?'

Nathalie took another drag. 'Balzac.'

That didn't sound right to Lara, but what did *she* know?

'You are Jack's cousin, yes?' Nathalie asked.

Lara nodded. 'Have you met all of Jack's family yet?'

'I know Madame de Trouville, yes. She is so charming.'

It wasn't the word Lara would use. She hadn't seen the woman since she was a child but she remembered a very cold, arrogant lady who complained about everything British.

'And Monsieur de Trouville,' Nathalie added. 'He, too, very charming.'

Not according to Jack, Lara thought, but instead she said, 'He's not Jack's real father, you know.'

Nathalie nodded. 'The real father, he comes to *le mariage*. I will be happy to meet him. Is he charming?'

Lara considered that. 'I don't know if *charming* is the right word. He's not nasty, or anything like that. But he's not very sociable.'

'He has nice home,' Nathalie said.

'I wouldn't know. Back when they lived near us, his place was OK. I haven't seen where he lives now. In another flat, I suppose.'

She'd spoken much too fast and Nathalie was clearly bewildered.

'He's a teacher,' Lara said carefully.

'Yes, Jack tells me. It is amusing for him?'

'Well, I don't know if it amuses him. He must like it because he's been a teacher for ever. That's what he does for a living.'

'Living,' Nathalie repeated. 'Yes, he is living.'

Lara gave up. 'Let's go and see our rooms.'

'I already see my room.' Nathalie took a mobile phone out of her bag. 'I stay here and make call.'

'OK, see you later.' Lara made her escape, and went into the château. Jack was just coming down the sweeping staircase.

'You're upstairs,' he told her. 'Room 109.'

'Thanks, Jack.'

Mounting the stairs, she couldn't help noticing that the interior of the château wasn't quite as impressive as the exterior. The chandelier that rose over the staircase was missing half its lights and the ornate carvings round the window she passed were cracked. Plaster was crumbling, wallpaper was peeling and the stairs creaked ominously. On the next floor, she walked across a threadbare carpet to the sound of voices coming from a room with an open door.

Standing in the doorway, she peered into the shabby room.

'Is this where we're staying?'

Alice and Harry, sitting side by side on a lower bed, nodded.

Horror filled her as she took in the two sets of bunk beds. '*All* of us?'

Again, the others nodded in unison. Harry looked

extremely glum. 'So I guess it's no hanky-panky this weekend.'

Lara glared at him. It was true, but did he have to say it so crudely?

Callum came into the room, and he'd caught Harry's remark. He had a more eloquent way of putting it.

'I think what my idiot friend means is that this is not exactly conducive to a romantic Parisian weekend.'

Alice nodded in agreement but Lara noticed that she didn't seem quite as annoyed as the others.

'Can we get another room?' Harry asked.

Callum shook his head. 'The building is under renovation; there are no more rooms available.'

Lara groaned. It looked like they were going to be stuck with this.

And it wasn't just a question of privacy – the room was tiny. She looked around. 'No wardrobe?'

'There are some hooks on the wall,' Alice told her.

'Where's the bathroom?'

'Down the hall,' Harry informed her.

Lara sank down on a lower bunk bed. 'No wonder it was cheap,' she said.

'Oh, well, *c'est la vie*,' Alice said. 'Looks like we'll be having a sleepover.'

'The mattresses aren't bad,' Callum pointed out.

Harry bounced up and down. 'Yeah, you're right. In fact, I'm going to have a little nap right now.' He climbed up the ladder to the top bunk. 'Hey, I like this! It reminds me of when I was a little kid and shared bunk beds with my brother.'

'Great,' Lara muttered.

'Do you want to go for a walk in the grounds?' Alice asked.

'Anything's better than hanging round in here,' Lara said.

'Cal? A walk?'

He shook his head and took out his mobile phone. 'I need to check in with the bank. I'll catch up with you.'

Walking down the creaky stairs, Lara continued to complain. 'I can't believe it. This was supposed to be a romantic getaway. *Not* a sleepover,' she added pointedly.

'I know,' Alice said. 'I'm sorry.'

Lara grimaced. 'For me and Harry. And for Callum too. I'm sure *he* had some expectations.'

'Probably,' Alice admitted. 'It's really a shame.'

'Then why aren't *you* looking more depressed?'

Alice sighed. 'I really do feel bad for you three. But I have to admit, it solves a problem for me. I'm just not sure I'm ready to take the big step with Callum.'

'Are you sure that's the only reason?'

Alice shrugged. 'Look, it's not easy. I mean, Jack was my first love. It feels weird to contemplate sleeping with Cal with Jack in the house.'

'It's not a house, it's a castle, and Jack isn't even on the same floor,' Lara declared.

'Still . . . It doesn't feel like the timing is right. Anyway, look on the bright side. It might not be the most romantic situation but we can still have a good time. We always have fun together, the four of us.'

More fun than she had alone with Cal? Lara wondered about this. She couldn't help feeling invested in the relationship. She'd been with Harry for quite some time when Callum moved to town. When Harry had introduced her, she immediately thought about Alice. Callum was a stranger in town and she knew he'd be hanging out with her and Harry. If Callum and Alice hit it off, so much the better!

She wanted their relationship to work. So far, they were getting along fine, but Lara hadn't detected any real passion. She was hoping that once Alice had got Jack out of her system for good, there would be a better chance for this to happen.

The girls walked round the château and what Lara saw in the gardens behind the castle almost compensated for her disappointment with the room. The grounds were spectacular. Small, circular flower beds filled with daffodils and tulips dotted the manicured lawn. The huge open space was surrounded by woodland, with enticing groomed paths that led into it. There was an enormous fountain, even larger than the one at the front, ornate iron benches and marble sculptures.

'What do you think of Nathalie?' Alice asked.

'She's OK, I suppose,' Lara replied, making no effort to hide her lack of enthusiasm. 'She smokes.'

'Really? She can't be pregnant then.'

Lara gazed at her thoughtfully. 'You sound like you're disappointed.'

'Not at all!' Alice replied. But Lara continued to look at her, knowing full well that Alice couldn't keep her feelings secret from *her*. And sure enough, under Lara's searching gaze, Alice gave in.

'I was thinking . . . if Nathalie was pregnant, that would explain why he was marrying her. But if she's *not* pregnant, that means . . .'

'He's in love with her?'

Alice nodded. 'Which is good,' she added. 'But it's . . . I don't know. Hard.' She managed a smile. 'It's another step in the direction of closure.'

Lara gave her friend a hug. 'Absolutely.'

'I'm surprised about the smoking though,' Alice

remarked. 'Jack always hated being around smokers.'

'He doesn't know she smokes. She asked me not to tell him. It's not just that though. She doesn't seem like Jack's type.'

Alice looked at her. 'What's Jack's type?'

'I don't know. But there's something about her . . . I think she's kind of cold.'

Alice shrugged. 'She was friendly enough on the boat.'

'Yeah, but just now when I was talking to her outside, she was a bit chilly with me.'

'We've only just met the girl!' Alice warned her. 'Give her a chance.'

Lara didn't answer. She'd been distracted and she stopped walking. 'Wow. Check *him* out. The guy standing by the fountain.'

'Nice,' Alice commented.

'That's an understatement.'

The tall, slender man seemed to be examining a statue of a naked woman which rose from the centre of the fountain. He wore a beautifully cut suit, grey, with a white shirt. He'd loosened his tie, and the top buttons of his shirt were undone. Lara found the whole look elegant and sexy at the same time.

He looked up and saw them. With a smile, he spoke in French.

Lara cursed the fact that she hadn't learned more in her language classes. She couldn't understand a word he said, but she tried to fake it. With a return smile, she said, '*Oui.*'

His smile broadened. 'You're English.'

'You can tell that from one word?' Lara asked.

'Not just that. I can tell by looking at you. You English girls . . . you have such a lovely, natural look. Beautiful skin, beautiful smiles.'

Lara was speechless. His compliment had been so easy and graceful. And he had the most gorgeous accent.

Alice had kept her wits about her. 'Thanks, but I think you're exaggerating.'

'Not at all,' he said. 'Surely you've been told this before.'

Alice laughed. 'Not really. But it's the first time we've been to France.'

'Ah, I see. I'm sure the men back in your own country admire you, but perhaps they are too . . . too reserved to tell you. A Frenchman can truly appreciate a woman and he is never too shy to express this. Are you here for the wedding?'

Finally, something Lara could respond to. 'Yes, Alice is an old friend of Jack's, and I'm his cousin. How do you know Jack?'

'We were students together, and now we are both *stagiaires* – apprentices – at the same law firm. And I am to be his best man at the wedding. Excuse me, I haven't introduced myself. My name is Christophe. Christophe de la Martinet.'

'I'm Lara and this is Alice.'

'*Enchanté, mesdemoiselles*. Delighted to meet you.'

Nathalie appeared from round the side of the château and approached the girls.

'I come to say, the dinner is at eight o'clock. It is not formal.' Her eyes swept over both the girls and seemed to say that the dinner was not that casual either.

'We're planning to change our clothes,' Lara assured her.

'*Bonjour*, Nathalie.'

Nathalie acknowledged the handsome boy with the briefest of glances. '*Bonjour*, Christophe.'

Lara caught a little twinkle in Christophe's eye as he proceeded to speak to Nathalie in French. She responded briefly, also in French. Then she gave a delicate little pouting expression and left them.

No love lost between them, Lara thought, and she wondered why.

'*Excusez-moi*,' Christophe said. 'I will change into something less formal.'

'See you at dinner,' Lara said.

He inclined his head in her direction. 'It will be my pleasure.'

Lara gazed after him in admiration. 'He's so French! In a good way, I mean.'

'Lovely manners,' Alice agreed. 'But did you see how Nathalie looked at him? I don't think they're great friends.'

'Maybe he's an ex-boyfriend,' Lara said.

'One that didn't give expensive presents,' Alice added, and told her about the conversation on the boat.

'That's what I meant when I said she wasn't Jack's type,' Lara said. 'She seems kind of shallow to me.'

'But if Christophe's an ex, then wouldn't it be strange for Jack to ask him to be best man?' Alice wondered.

Lara shrugged. 'Maybe boys deal with exes better than girls. Or maybe he's such a great friend that Jack doesn't care. Anyway, I want Harry to meet Christophe.'

'You think they'll get on?'

Lara grinned. 'Hardly. But maybe he could give Harry a lesson in manners. Come on, let's get ready for dinner.'

Chapter Seven

Opening her eyes, for one brief moment Alice thought she was a child again, having a sleepover with her best friend. But the best friend asleep on the other bed wasn't a child, and neither was she. Alice raised her eyes. On the bed above Lara's she could see a mound of blankets under which Harry was sleeping. And since she heard nothing coming from the bunk above *her*, she assumed Callum was sound asleep too. They'd all been up pretty late the night before.

Dinner had been very pleasant – roast chicken, green beans, salads, delicious cheeses she couldn't even identify, and not an oyster or strange animal organ in sight. Even Harry couldn't complain. In fact, Harry had been the life and soul of the party, and Alice was enormously grateful – since there were only seven of them, and since Callum now knew that Jack was her ex, the conversation had been a bit stilted to start with. But Harry had entertained them with hysterically funny stories about a recent *fête* in his home village. Tales of barrel rolling and a competition among farmers regarding vegetables that looked like famous people had them all laughing. The very best was his story about the three-legged race he'd run with his kid sister during which his trousers fell down.

Nathalie had barely understood anything, even though Jack provided translations in his impeccable French. Alice noticed how attentive he was to her, always encouraging her to eat more. There had been wine on the table, but when Christophe began to pour it, Jack put his hand over Nathalie's glass and shook his head. So maybe she really was pregnant.

It was interesting to watch Christophe too. He confirmed every stereotype of the French man – beautiful table manners, holding chairs out for the girls, not allowing them to pour their own wine, making eye contact with everyone who spoke. And his concept of 'casual' wasn't quite like the others'. Callum, Harry and Jack all wore jeans and T-shirts. Christophe wore immaculately pressed trousers, a crisp pale-blue shirt and a dark cardigan over his shoulders. Alice was amused to see how Lara's eyes darted back and forth between Christophe's smart-casual look and Harry's T-shirt, which commemorated a Red Hot Chili Peppers gig from years earlier and bore some suspicious marks which were undoubtedly souvenirs of meals eaten.

Nathalie left the table as soon as dinner was over but the others stayed up late, moving to a sitting room with comfortable sofas and taking the wine with them. Alice sat close to Cal. He put his arm round her and she rested her head on his chest. She often sat like this with him; it was comfortable and cosy. At one point, she caught Jack looking at them. She smiled and cuddled closer to Callum.

When they'd finally retired for the evening, everyone was so exhausted that the lack of privacy in the bedroom was insignificant – they fell asleep immediately.

So far, so good, Alice thought as she stretched and sat up. No awkward moments – not yet anyway. Slipping out of bed, she wrapped herself in a robe, took up her towel, wash bag and clothes, and left the room.

At least the bathrooms in the château were up to date. There were three toilet cubicles, a machine dispensing feminine hygiene products, three showers and plenty of space for dressing and undressing. This was something else Alice wasn't ready to do in front of Callum, or Harry either, for that matter.

Back in the room, Callum and Harry were just climbing down from their bunks. There were some mumbled 'good mornings' and they left for the bathroom. Alice sat down on Lara's bed and gave her a gentle nudge.

'Rise and shine,' she said.

Lara opened one eye. 'What time is it?'

'Nine thirty,' Alice told her. 'We need to get moving.'

Lara yawned and stretched. 'What's the plan?'

'Jack said Nathalie is going to show us round Paris. And if I understood correctly, she wants us to meet her at ten.'

'Two days before her wedding? Shouldn't she have more important things to do?'

'I don't get it either,' Alice agreed. 'I imagine other guests are going to start arriving. You'd think she'd want to be here to greet them. Maybe that's what Jack's going to do.'

'So Nathalie's going to be our travel guide.' Lara frowned. 'She doesn't strike me as a culture vulture.'

'Well, at least she'll know her way around,' Alice said. 'We're taking the train into Paris, just us girls. I don't know what the boys are going to do.'

'I do,' Lara said. 'Harry told me they're going to play golf.'

'Golf? Callum doesn't play golf!'

Lara grinned. 'Neither does Harry. But it seems that when they were kids they used to play the pitch-and-putt course a lot. They've got some stupid notion of reliving their youth and Jack told them about a golf course near here where they can rent clubs. Of course, they don't want us coming along to watch them make fools of themselves.'

'I don't care as long as they're back in time to meet us. Jack's mother and stepfather are hosting dinner at some trendy restaurant.'

'That presents a wardrobe question,' Lara remarked. 'What works for sightseeing all day and then going to a restaurant?'

Alice stood up. 'I chose this.'

Lara took in Alice's simple olive-green wrap dress and nodded. 'OK, I can do something like that.' She went to her suitcase and picked out a pretty violet shirt dress.

'And I suggest wearing flats and carrying heels in our bags,' Alice recommended.

Breakfast was laid out in the room where they'd had dinner the night before. There were gorgeous flaky croissants, baguettes, a variety of jams, orange juice and coffee. Christophe was already there with Jack, standing by the buffet and selecting their food. They were deep in conversation when the girls arrived.

'I'm being instructed as to the responsibilities of the best man,' Christophe told the girls with a charming smile. 'I have to give a toast at the dinner tonight, prepare the playlist for dancing at the reception, carry the rings and escort the maid of honour. A lot of responsibility, yes? And I thought all I would have to do is stand by his side.'

'Well, that *is* your number-one job,' Jack told him. 'And making sure my tie is straight.'

'And getting you to the altar.' Lara added. 'I saw a film once about a wedding where the best man talked the groom out of getting married at the very last minute.'

'That won't happen here,' Jack laughed. 'Christophe has been very supportive.'

Alice just happened to be looking at Christophe as Jack spoke. A thin smile, almost unpleasant, made a brief appearance on his face. It was a curious reaction, she thought. And it didn't express any great enthusiasm for the upcoming marriage. Maybe he *was* Nathalie's ex.

They sat down and, moments later, Callum and Harry joined them. Harry looked over the spread and sighed.

'I suppose I should have known it wouldn't be a fry-up.'

'What is a fry-up?' Christophe asked.

Harry launched into a rapturous description of the full English breakfast. Christophe could deal with the eggs, sausage and bacon, but when Harry got to the beans, mushrooms and tomatoes, he was appalled.

'You eat all this for breakfast?'

'Not every day,' Lara assured him quickly. 'And personally, I much prefer a continental breakfast, like this.'

'Since when?' Harry asked. 'You're always thrilled when I do you a fry-up!'

They'd all just taken their plates to the table when Nathalie appeared with another girl. The companion had none of Nathalie's classic French taste. Her hair was a highly artificial red and she wore leopard-skin leggings with a sequinned top that barely reached her waist. And she wore heavy-duty make-up, eyes outlined in black, and fuchsia lips. But clearly, they were good friends – they entered the room with their arms linked.

'Here comes the maid of honour,' Jack murmured.

Once again, Alice caught a glimpse of distaste cross Christophe's face. This time, though, she thought she understood it. The maid of honour did not look like the kind of woman the elegant Frenchman would want to escort.

Nevertheless, he rose as they approached, and so did

Jack. Callum nudged Harry, and they got up too, although Harry looked like he didn't know why.

Nathalie and Jack kissed, and then Nathalie began speaking to him in French, but he stopped her.

'Don't forget our guests! Speak English. Why don't you introduce everyone?'

Nathalie looked pained, but she obliged. 'Everyone, this is Claudine. We go to Paris now.'

'Alice and Lara haven't finished breakfast yet, Nathalie.'

Nathalie looked at him blankly. 'They come with us?'

'Don't you remember?' Jack asked. 'We talked about it last night. You said you'd take them into Paris and show them round. Then we'll all meet up at the restaurant for dinner.'

Alice couldn't see Nathalie's face but the slump of her shoulders told her Nathalie had completely forgotten, and wasn't thrilled at being reminded. But she responded sweetly.

'But of course, mon amour! They come with us.'

Alice had thought the outfits she and Lara had selected for the day were just right – they'd be comfortable tramping around museums, but they would look perfectly appropriate for dinner in a nice restaurant. Nathalie seemed to only have taken the evening into account. She wore a short black skirt with a matching fitted jacket. On her feet were sky-high stiletto heels.

'How will you walk all day in *those*?' Lara asked Nathalie.

'We take taxis,' Nathalie replied.

Alice didn't like the sound of that. Her limited budget for the weekend wouldn't extend to expensive taxi rides. But then Nathalie said something in French to Jack, and he took out his wallet.

Speaking in English, he said, 'I'd rather you use this money to buy some good walking shoes.'

Nathalie smiled. She gave him another, more lingering kiss this time, and accepted the money.

Privately, Alice agreed with Jack. Even if they took taxis from one sight to the next, big museums required a lot of walking and she doubted that Nathalie would be comfortable trekking through the Louvre in those stilettos.

After breakfast – during which Nathalie only picked at her croissant and put infinitesimal bits in her mouth – Jack drove them to the railway station. They only had to wait a few minutes before the train came along. Once they were settled in their seats, Alice took out her guidebook.

'So here's what I thought we could do today. First there's the Louvre, of course, and then the Orsay

Museum has a wonderful collection of Impressionist art. And there's the Picasso Museum—'

'Is only for tourists.' Nathalie did her poofy lip thing, this time accompanied by some nose wrinkling.

'We *are* tourists,' Lara pointed out.

Nathalie turned away and looked out of the window. Claudine was a little more informative.

'There is no time for museums,' she told them. 'We have more important places to see.'

'Like what?' Alice asked.

'You'll see,' Claudine replied with a cat-like smile. She took a mirror out of her purse and applied an unnecessary additional layer of hot-pink lipstick.

She was being very mysterious, Alice thought. Obviously, the girls had already made plans for the day. Maybe they knew some less well-known places. She was a little disappointed that they wouldn't hit the Louvre, but maybe having a day with real Parisiennes would be even more interesting.

'Your English is very good,' she told Claudine. 'Did you take courses at university?'

'University?' Claudine laughed, and poked Nathalie. Nathalie spoke softly and very quickly to her, in French. Claudine nodded, giggled again and responded to Alice.

'I do not go to university, like Nathalie. I learn English

from friends.' She began rattling off names. 'At school, there was Max, exchange student from the United States. Then, on holiday, I met a boy from England, Nigel. Maybe you know him?'

'Nigel What?' Lara asked.

'Oh, I do not remember his last name. Now I have Bruce, Australian boyfriend. You do not speak French?'

'I took a course once but I guess I didn't learn much,' Lara said. 'I've barely understood a word since I've been here.'

'If you want to improve, find a French lover,' Claudine advised. 'It is the best way.'

'I'll remember that,' Lara assured her. Alice had to look the other way and bite her lower lip to keep from laughing out loud.

Claudine turned to Nathalie. 'We speak English today.'

'English,' Nathalie muttered, as if it was a dirty word. 'You are like Jack, he want that I speak English. I prefer to speak French.'

Alice looked at her curiously. It seemed to her that Nathalie had been more pleasant at the château. Maybe her nerves were on edge, getting married in two days, meeting all these new people . . .

'I think Jack just wants you to feel comfortable when you're living in Britain,' she suggested.

Nathalie's forehead puckered, as if she didn't understand. Alice tried to put it another way.

'After Jack graduates, when you move to England, you'll need to speak English.'

Nathalie shrugged. 'Maybe we move to England, maybe we stay in France. The mother of Jack, she has very grand apartment.'

'But would you want to live with them?' Alice asked. 'Would Jack want to do that?'

'In England, there is an estate, yes?'

Alice and Lara spoke simultaneously. 'An estate?' They looked at each other, and Alice was sure they were both thinking the same thing. Back home, Jack and his father had lived in Hartfield Estate, a row of modest, newly built garden apartments. Should they try to explain that a housing estate was not a stately home?

'My English boyfriend, he had mansion in London,' Claudine reported proudly.

Alice thought of the hundreds of apartment blocks in cities that were called Something Mansions. Obviously, the girls didn't understand British property terminology. She really didn't want to be the one to destroy their illusions. Nathalie would learn it soon enough on her own.

Nathalie took out her little make-up bag and poked

around inside. Then she frowned and asked Claudine something in French.

'English!' Claudine reminded her.

'I do not know word!' Nathalie snapped. 'What is English for *mascara*?'

Lara jumped in. 'Mascara.'

Nathalie looked at her through narrowed eyes. 'Merci,' she hissed.

When they arrived at the station in Paris, Alice made a pitch for the Paris tube system, the Métro, but Nathalie ignored her and led the way to the queue for taxis. Fortunately, they didn't have to wait long. As they piled into the taxi, Nathalie gave the driver instructions in French.

Hoping Lara might have understood a word or two, Alice asked in a whisper, 'Do you know where we're going?'

'Not a clue,' Lara whispered back.

Nathalie turned and looked at Alice in an almost accusatory way, and Alice wondered if she thought her rude for whispering to Lara. Nathalie, however, seemed to have no problem with that practice. She began speaking very softly to Claudine in French.

Alice turned her head so she could watch Paris passing by through the window. It was sunny today, the weather was mild and she wished she could be outside walking in the beautiful city.

The taxi turned on to a street that was lined with shops. Above the shops, the age-darkened white-ish buildings displayed windows with geraniums hanging from wrought-iron balconies. It was lovely, but Alice didn't see anything that looked important or any signs for museums. They stopped at a corner, and as Nathalie paid the driver, Alice took note of the street name – rue du Faubourg Saint-Honoré.

Nathalie led them across the street to a shoe shop and Alice could see immediately that sturdy walking boots were not exactly what she had in mind.

There were shoes, of course – most of them with incredibly high stiletto heels. There were shoes perched in cut-out cubbyholes along one wall, displayed like works of art. There was a Ferris wheel, where high-heeled shoes went around in a circle. Some of them looked more like sculptures than shoes, strange shapes decorated with tufts of fur, enormous buckles, flowers.

'The best shoes in Paris,' Claudine announced gleefully. She picked up a sequinned platform sandal and cradled it like a baby. 'Beautiful, yes?'

Lara picked up a more traditional shoe covered in a leopard print. 'I like this,' she said. To a passing saleswoman, she asked, 'Excuse me, can you tell me how much these are?'

Fortunately, the woman understood and answered her in English. Even so, Alice wasn't so sure she'd heard correctly when the woman said, 'One thousand, two hundred euros.'

Lara stared at the woman. Then she turned to Alice. 'What's that in pounds?'

Alice took out her mobile phone and clicked on the currency conversion application. 'One thousand and fifty-four.'

Very, very carefully, Lara replaced the shoe in its cubbyhole. 'Who would pay over a thousand pounds for a pair of shoes?' she asked in complete wonderment.

Nathalie gave her a contemptuous look. She turned over the shoe she was holding and tapped the red sole. 'Is Christian Louboutin!' She turned to the saleswoman and spoke. The saleswoman nodded and hurried away.

'I think she just asked to see a pair in her size,' Lara whispered to Alice in awe.

Alice made sure both the French girls were out of earshot before she spoke. 'Maybe Jack *has* taken after his mother. You know what I mean?'

'Marrying for money?' Lara shook her head. 'She's an

orphan and she works in the uni canteen to pay her tuition fees.'

They watched as the saleswoman knelt before Nathalie and helped her into the sequinned platforms. Nathalie rose and took a few steps towards a mirror, where she stopped to admire them. Alice and Lara joined her there.

'Do you buy all your shoes here, Nathalie?' Alice asked.

Claudine glanced at Nathalie knowingly before answering for her. 'Not yet. But someday soon, we think.'

Lara pulled Alice aside. 'How can she afford shoes like that?' she whispered in Alice's ear.

Alice didn't know. 'Wishful thinking? Maybe she's coming into an inheritance.'

Lara shook her head. 'Orphan, remember?'

Alice considered this. 'Maybe she just likes to dream.' She just hoped this dream didn't go on too much longer though. Her own curiosity about outrageous shoes at outrageous prices was fading fast.

Nathalie sauntered towards them and actually spoke. 'You do not try on shoes?'

Alice forced a smile. 'They're not really my style, Nathalie.'

Nathalie glanced down at Alice's flats. 'No, I see that.'

Fortunately, Nathalie didn't intend to try on every

shoe in the shop. After two more pairs, Nathalie reluctantly allowed them to leave.

'There's a taxi stand,' Lara pointed out.

Nathalie glanced at her dismissively. 'We do not need taxi. We stay on this street.'

'This is a good French experience for you!' Claudine declared. 'That way, there is Yves Saint Laurent. Down that way, Lanvin. A bit further, you can see Prada.'

'I think Prada is Italian,' Alice said.

Claudine raised her eyebrows. 'Really? Well, we are all Europe now. Not you, of course.'

Alice raised her eyebrows. 'The UK is in the European Union, Claudine!'

'Yes? But you have strange money.'

Alice didn't particularly want to get into a debate about currency. 'Isn't the Louvre near here?' she asked to change the subject.

'Perhaps, I don't know. But after this street, we can go to avenue Montaigne, and you will see . . .' She paused dramatically. 'Dior! And Dolce and Gabbana! Also Italian, but very nice. And here . . .' She stopped walking. 'Hermès! You know Hermès?'

'I've heard of it,' Alice said carefully. She'd seen a piece in a magazine recently about Victoria Beckham's passion for the Hermès Birkin bag, one of the most expensive handbags in the world. Posh had one in every colour. Somehow, Alice didn't think she'd be seeing anything affordable in *this* shop either.

But Nathalie marched right in with Claudine. Alice looked at Lara and shrugged. Obviously they had no say in the matter, and they followed.

Alice had a recurring dream – a nightmare, really – where she would find herself walking down a high street somewhere and suddenly realize she was only wearing a threadbare nightshirt that barely covered her knickers. She was reminded of this when she entered Hermès. She wasn't quite as inappropriately dressed here but she felt very out of place.

Every customer looked as if she had stepped out of the pages of *Vogue*. Beautifully coiffed and made up, they wore jewellery that was clearly expensive, and even on this mild day, several wore fur coats. Designer bags that Alice recognized from magazines dangled from their arms. She noticed that several customers carried little dogs, the kind that looked more like toys than animals. They probably wore expensive perfumes too, though she didn't get close enough to anyone to smell them. Still, there was a scent in the air – the shop reeked of big money.

Once again, they were entertained by Claudine's little

moans of delight as she showed them a silk scarf that cost even more than the red-soled shoes. The items were all beautifully displayed, and Alice supposed that a real fashion victim could consider this to be a museum of sorts, but personally, she'd rather be looking at the *Mona Lisa*.

Nathalie was engaged in what appeared to be an intense conversation with a salesman.

'She is asking about the waiting list for the Birkin bag,' Claudine translated for them, and went to join in this important discussion.

'I hope we're not going to spend the whole day shopping,' Alice said to Lara.

'Who's shopping?' Lara asked. 'All we can do in these places is look at stuff we can't afford. This is crazy! We only have three days in Paris, and Sunday's the wedding so we can't do any sightseeing then. Let's split.'

'What do you mean?'

'We leave Nathalie to her wishful thinking and go and see something interesting.'

Alice shook her head. 'We can't do that. What would Jack say if we dumped his fiancée and took off on our own? I don't want him to think . . . you know.'

'That we don't like his girlfriend?'

'He might think it's jealousy or something.' She

glanced over at Nathalie. Talking about a handbag was making her more animated and happy than she'd been all day. 'I'll tell you this though. I'm beginning to think your snap judgement about her was right on target.'

Lara nodded vigorously. 'She really is kind of awful. I can't figure out what he sees in her. She's got to be pregnant, Alice. What other reason could there be?'

Alice wasn't sure. 'Maybe he sees something in her we don't. "Opposites attract" and all that. Look at you and Harry. Or maybe Jack's changed. A *lot*.'

Lara frowned. 'Whatever. But I don't want to spend the whole day looking at luxuries that are out of my league.'

Alice agreed. 'Let me try talking to her, and ask if we can do something else.'

She made a concerted effort to communicate their concern when they finally got out of Hermès. 'Nathalie, this is all very . . . fascinating. But we're only here for three days and we'd really like to see something more . . . more historical. Cultural.'

Nathalie looked at her coldly. 'Now I show you a place very important in French history and culture. It is close to here, on rue Cambon.'

It was only a five-minute walk before they found themselves in front of a building where the door was decorated with intertwining letter Cs. In the windows, mannequins displayed exquisite clothes.

'Is Chanel,' Nathalie said with reverence. From her tone, she could have been standing in front of a famed cathedral. 'You will want souvenir of France to take home. Chanel is very French. Maybe you find something here.'

Lara let out an exasperated groan. 'I was thinking more of a plastic Eiffel Tower or something like that.'

'You do not want to buy French clothes?' Claudine asked in disbelief.

That was when it hit Alice – Nathalie and her friend thought they were rich! Alice tried to explain.

'Nathalie, we can't afford anything from Chanel! We're students, just like you and Jack! We don't have a lot of money.'

Nathalie sneered. 'But you are not like me. You have families.'

Alice tried to drum up some compassion for the poor orphan, and she spoke gently. 'Our families aren't rich, Nathalie.'

'But you are friends with Jack.'

Now Alice was bewildered. What did that have to do with anything?

Lara broke in. 'I'm getting hungry,' she announced.

Claudine turned to Nathalie. 'Hotel Costes?'

Nathalie took out her wallet and checked the contents. Then she looked at Lara and Alice. 'You have real money? Euros?'

'Pounds are real money, Nathalie,' Lara declared in annoyance. 'But yes, we have euros too.'

But Alice was thinking about something else. A hotel restaurant? 'Nathalie, I don't want to go anywhere expensive. I saw a good-looking sandwich place on our way here, and on my map it looks like there's a park nearby.'

From Nathalie's expression, Alice could see that the concept of a picnic was as foreign to her as pounds sterling. She muttered something to Claudine in French and they started walking.

'I caught the word "anglaise",' Lara whispered. 'I think she just insulted us.'

Alice could believe it.

They picked up sandwiches and drinks, and walked to the Tuileries garden, which turned out to be opposite the Louvre. Alice would at least get a look at the exterior of the famed museum.

On another side of the park was the rue de Rivoli, a beautiful street lined with vaulted arcades.

'This is lovely,' Alice said. 'Do people live in these buildings?'

'Yes, is very chic,' Claudine told them.

Suddenly Nathalie looked at Lara and Alice with something that almost looked like interest. 'You know Jack very well, yes?'

'We're cousins,' Lara said.

'Yes, I know, but *you* . . .' She looked at Alice. 'You were lovers. And lovers, they know best.'

'Oh, we were never lovers,' Alice said quickly. 'I mean, we never made love. We were just kids.'

'But you know what his, his . . . his *goût*.'

'I don't know what that means,' Alice said. Her guidebook had a small French–English dictionary in the back and she handed it over to Nathalie.

'Ah! Here is word in English. You know his *taste*.'

'You mean, like in food?' Alice thought back. 'He used to eat a lot of kebabs.'

Nathalie brushed that aside. 'I don't know what this is, kebab. I want to know this. Jack, he will like to live here?'

'Here? You mean, in Paris?'

Nathalie waved her hand to indicate the handsome buildings that lined the park. 'Here. Rue de Rivoli.'

Lara jumped into the discussion. 'Well, who wouldn't? It's pretty. But I think Jack really wants to come back to England.'

'Ah yes, the estate,' Nathalie murmured.

Once again, Alice and Lara exchanged looks. 'Maybe you can live in two places,' Alice suggested.

'Yeah,' Lara chimed in. 'A city place in Paris, a country estate in England.'

Alice hid her smile. Let Nathalie hang on to her fantasies – she'd learn the truth sooner or later.

'You are finished with sandwich?' Nathalie asked. 'We can shop now.'

'The Louvre is right here,' Alice pointed out, but Nathalie shook her head.

'I must find pearls for my wedding gown.'

Alice gave up. If Jack knew she'd interfered with Nathalie's wedding needs, he really might get the wrong impression. And if she suggested splitting up, he'd think she was bitter about his marriage, maybe that she resented it. She couldn't win.

'We go to Place Vendôme?' Claudine asked hopefully. 'At Place Vendôme, there are great jewellery shops.' she explained to the English girls. 'Or perhaps we go to Cartier?'

Nathalie actually spoke partly in English. 'Jack, he does not give me so much money. We go to *dépôt vente*.'

A *dépôt vente* turned out to be a second-hand shop, but it was nothing like the Oxfam back home. There were second-hand clothes and jewellery from top designers, and the prices weren't that cheap either. But while Nathalie and Claudine pored over the jewellery, Lara found a reasonably priced dress to try on, and Alice saw something that tempted *her* – a red silk tunic with gold embroidery that would turn an ordinary pair of jeans into a real outfit. A few broken threads had reduced the price to something almost affordable.

They emerged from the dressing room to check themselves out in the large mirror.

'I *love* this!' Lara squealed. She twirled around in the front of the mirror. 'It's like the perfect little black dress! I swear, I think I actually look French. I'm getting it.' After preening for a couple of moments, she went back into the dressing room.

Alice was pleased with the red tunic too, and she knew Callum loved her in red. Nathalie and Claudine came over to look at her.

'Is nice for you,' Claudine said. 'What do you think, Nathalie?'

'Yes, good for you,' Nathalie agreed. 'It hides the . . . what is the word in English?' She put her hands on her hips.

Lara emerged from the dressing room just in time to hear this. 'Alice doesn't have big hips!'

Nathalie shrugged. 'Maybe not so big as most English girls.'

Alice couldn't help shooting her a sharp look but managed to hold her tongue. 'Thank you, Nathalie,' she said sweetly. 'I like this top very much.'

'You buy?'

Alice looked at the price tag again, and mentally debated. 'I don't know . . . it's not cheap.'

'Your boyfriend can buy for you?'

'Callum? I'd never ask him to buy me clothes!'

'But why not?' Nathalie asked. 'I ask Jack, he buy me clothes sometimes. He pay for my wedding gown.' She held up a string of pearls. 'And this.'

Lara gaped.

'They are not real,' Claudine assured them.

Nathalie glared at her before turning back to the others. 'And I need also, how do you say . . . for the head.'

'Veil?' Alice asked.

'No . . . like a crown.'

Lara continued to gape. 'You're planning to wear a crown?'

'I think she means a tiara,' Alice told her.

Nathalie nodded. 'Yes, that is word. Tiara. I must have this. But I cannot buy today. I forget to ask Jack for *carte de crédit*.'

For what felt like the gazillionth time that day, Alice and Lara exchanged looks. As soon as Nathalie and Claudine went to the till at the other side of the shop, they huddled.

'Do you think Jack actually buys her clothes?' Lara wondered. 'He's a student! Where does the money come from?'

'His mother, probably,' Alice said. 'By way of his rich stepfather.' It bothered her, to think of Jack taking money from a man he didn't like. The Jack she knew wouldn't do something like that. He really *had* changed.

'But even so, don't you think it's a little creepy, letting your boyfriend buy you clothes? OK, maybe for a birthday present or Christmas. But all the time? It seems kind of, I don't know . . .'

Alice did. 'Like she's his mistress or something. Well, maybe it's a French thing. And Jack's been here for two years. He must be in touch with his French side.'

Nathalie came back with a little bag. Her mobile rang, and she answered it. '*Allo? Oui. D'accord, mon amour.*' She tossed the phone back in her bag. 'Jack say we meet now. We have tea.'

'Wonderful!' Alice exclaimed. She was probably overreacting, and she wasn't surprised that both Nathalie and Lara looked at her oddly. But she was just so happy to know there was something about Jack that was still English.

Chapter Eight

The tea *salon*, Angelina, was right on the elegant rue de Rivoli, and pretty impressive inside too. Entering the restaurant, Alice admired the marble-topped tables, the gilded ironwork and mirrored walls. There were several people waiting to be seated, but then she spotted Jack on his way to fetch them. They all went through the whole cheek-kissing thing again.

'We're over here,' he said, and led them to the largest table in the centre of the room. Alice was relieved to see that Callum was there too, along with Harry and Christophe. The boys got up and they kissed more cheeks. Alice sat down next to Callum and gave him a kiss on the lips.

'Get something nice?' Callum asked, eyeing her bag.

'In your favourite colour,' Alice replied. 'How was golf? Who won?'

Callum and Harry looked at each other and grinned. 'We forgot to keep score,' Harry confessed.

'We've grown up,' Callum added ruefully. 'That never would have happened back in the old pitch-and-putt days.'

'And real golf isn't that much fun anyway,' Harry told them.

'I don't suppose you bought any walking shoes,' Jack asked Nathalie.

'No, but I have this!' She showed him the string of pearls. 'Not real,' she said mournfully.

The price tag was still attached, and Jack's eyes widened.

'Wow! That's a lot of money for fake pearls. So you got this instead of a tiara?'

'Oh, I must have tiara too!' Nathalie said. 'I find tiara tomorrow.'

Jack frowned but he said nothing.

'I buy nothing,' Claudine said sadly. 'I must find English boyfriend like Nathalie.'

'I'm glad you got to spend time with Alice and Lara,' Jack told Nathalie. 'I want you to know my friends from back home.'

Nathalie smiled brightly. 'Oh, I adore your friends, Jack!'

Lara looked as if she was about to choke, and Alice

tried to compensate. 'Yes, we had a great time together,' she lied.

'What did you get?' Harry asked Lara.

'You'll see. I'm going to change before dinner.' She sighed. 'Not that you'll notice.'

'That cannot be true,' Christophe declared. 'A woman like you will always be noticed.'

Lara beamed at Christophe and then looked pointedly at Harry. Harry didn't catch the look – he was too busy studying the menu.

'What's a Mont Blanc?' he asked.

'It is a little taste of heaven,' Christophe told him. 'A delicate puréed chestnut cream which rests atop a light meringue that will melt in your mouth.'

Harry stared at him as if he'd just heard gibberish. 'OK. I, um, think I'll stick to chocolate cake.'

'Oh, Harry,' Lara groaned. 'Must you be so – so plebian?'

Alice couldn't decide what to get, everything on the menu sounded so delicious – at least, the items she could understand did.

'*Chocolat chaud*,' she murmured and smiled.

Hot chocolate, her addiction. Jack used to tease her about that, how she'd order hot chocolate even in the summer. At that very moment, he turned to her.

'I remember how much you love hot chocolate, but you've never had a hot chocolate like they serve it here. If you're not dead set on tea, you have to order it.'

For a moment, she couldn't speak. When she found her voice, she said, 'Yes, that's what I'll have.'

'And a Mont Blanc,' Christophe declared. 'You must. And do not look at the price. I invite you. All of you.'

'Oh, that's not necessary,' Callum protested.

'I insist,' Christophe said firmly. 'Lara, what would you like?'

'I'm not sure. I can't figure out what half of these things are.'

'I will ask for an English menu,' Christophe said immediately, and rose.

'He's so nice!' Lara said to the others. 'Such a gentleman.'

Callum looked concerned. 'Can he really afford to treat us all? Isn't he a student like you, Jack?'

'Not like me,' Jack said. 'You should see his apartment. Totally *not* student digs.' He turned to Alice. 'Remember when I told you how the French make a big deal about having a name with "de" in it? He's Christophe *de* la Martinet. But his family still has the money to go with the name.'

Alice saw an unreadable expression cross Nathalie's

face. Did she not know Christophe was wealthy? Lara must have noticed it too.

'I'm surprised Nathalie doesn't go after *him*,' she whispered in Alice's ear.

Christophe returned with the English menu and handed it to Lara with a flourish. '*Voilà, belle mademoiselle.*'

Lara clearly understood *that*, because she actually blushed. Alice couldn't remember the last time she'd seen Lara go pink like that.

The waitress came to their table and they placed their orders. Then Lara turned to Christophe.

'You and Jack must be good mates.'

Christophe was taken aback. 'Mates?'

Jack laughed. 'He's thinking of "mates" as a husband and wife, Lara. We use the word for friends,' he assured Christophe.

'Ah. Then yes, we are very good mates. We study together and we enjoy each other's company socially too. Just last weekend I attended a concert with Jack and Nathalie.' He sighed. 'Of course, it is not always easy to be with this couple.'

Alice glanced at Nathalie. Clearly she wasn't following the English conversation. She was examining her perfectly manicured nails.

'Why isn't it easy?' Lara asked.

'Because I am a lonely *célibataire*, a bachelor,' he replied. 'To be with a happy couple like Jack and Nathalie . . . well, I cannot help but feel envy.'

'Oh, give me a break,' Jack said with a grin. 'You never lack for female companionship.'

Christophe smiled. 'But a pleasant date is no substitute for true love. Don't you agree, Nathalie?'

Nathalie looked up. '*Comment?*'

Christophe repeated what he'd said in French. But it was almost as if she still didn't understand. She just stared at him through narrowed eyes. She really doesn't like him, Alice thought, and she wondered why. Did she not like having him hang round with them? Maybe she felt like she and Jack didn't have enough time alone.

Their food arrived and everything looked fabulous. Alice's hot chocolate was thick and dark, and it was served with a bowl of whipped cream on the side, so she could add as much as she liked.

'Ohmigod, this is lovely,' she moaned.

'Try the Mont Blanc,' Christophe suggested.

She did, and it was like nothing she'd had before, a little taste of heaven. Even Harry couldn't find anything to complain about.

'OK, I've finally found something in France that I'm

happy to eat,' he announced. 'That coffee this morning at the café on the golf course, it was *bitter*.'

'That's how they drink it here, Harry,' Lara muttered through gritted teeth. Then to Christophe, 'Personally, I think the coffee here in France is delicious.'

Christophe acknowledged the compliment with a slight bow of his head. 'On behalf of France, I thank you for your appreciation.'

Claudine was eating *mousse au chocolat*. 'Nathalie, you must try this, it is the best I ever eat and there is too much.'

Nathalie, who had only ordered a cup of tea, shook her head.

'Didn't you want anything, Nathalie?' asked Jack.

Nathalie shook her head.

'I do not want to be fat.'

'Do not worry, Nathalie,' Christophe interjected. 'Even if you are fat, I am certain Jack will marry you.'

At that, Nathalie gave him the coldest look Alice had seen to date. Everyone noticed it and there was an uncomfortable silence. Callum tried to fill it.

'Are many more of your wedding guests staying at the château?' he asked.

'An aunt and uncle coming from England, and my father,' Jack told him. 'Most of the guests live in Paris, so they'll just come on Sunday for the ceremony and the reception. Christophe is the only local one staying at the château.'

Lara looked at Christophe curiously. 'Jack says you have a really nice flat. Why are you staying at the château? No offence, Jack, but the rooms aren't exactly, uh, *magnifique*.'

'But perfectly comfortable,' Callum said quickly.

Under the table, Alice took his hand and squeezed it. It couldn't be easy for him here, among all these strangers, and he was being so kind.

'The château's in the process of renovation,' Jack told them. 'The two finished rooms are pretty upscale, and a lot more expensive than the rooms you guys have. Christophe's got one, Nathalie and I are in the other. It's part of Mother's wedding gift, along with the reception.'

Nathalie beamed at him. 'Your parents are so very kind. Already, I think of them as *maman* and *papa*.'

'You haven't met my father yet,' Jack reminded her.

'But Monsieur de Trouville, he is like a father to you,' Nathalie declared.

Jack just rolled his eyes.

It occurred to Alice that Nathalie's knowledge of English seemed to vary – sometimes she was oblivious to what was being said, other times she understood perfectly. Or maybe she just tuned out when the conversation wasn't interesting her. She decided she'd better warn Lara that maybe the girl understood more than they thought, and Lara should watch what she said in front of her.

'In any case,' Christophe said, 'even if I had to sleep in one of the more humble rooms, I would stay at the château. On an important occasion like this, a man needs his closest friend, yes? His mate?' He turned to Nathalie. 'And when does *your* family arrive, Nathalie?'

Alice bit her lip and looked anxiously at Nathalie. The girl had stiffened, and her lips formed a thin line as she glared at Christophe.

Jack spoke quietly. 'Nathalie's parents passed away, Christophe, a long time ago. You know that.'

Christophe made an apologetic face. 'Oh, of course, I have completely forgotten. I am so terribly sorry. Do forgive me, Nathalie.'

He was certainly being contrite, Alice thought. But his words didn't seem to impress Nathalie. She didn't acknowledge the apology, and continued to glare at him with what was by now unmistakable hatred.

Another moment of silence fell over the table. Finally, Callum spoke.

'Well . . . what shall we do for the rest of the afternoon?'

Jack shot him a look of gratitude, and Alice was pleased. Callum was always so good at dealing with awkward situations.

Nathalie spoke up. 'I want to look for – now I forget, what is the word again? Ah yes. Tiara. Perhaps we go to Place Vendôme?'

'I think Place Vendôme may be a bit beyond our means, Nathalie,' Jack said gently.

'But I am bride! I must have tiara!'

'Is that the law in France?' Lara asked, her eyes twinkling mischievously.

'We'll find something like that tomorrow,' Jack told her. 'Today, we need to entertain our guests. What would you guys like to do?' Jack was speaking to the group, but his eyes were on Alice, so she replied.

'I was going to suggest the Louvre, but the weather's so nice, maybe we should do something outdoors.'

'How about the Eiffel Tower?' Lara offered.

Jack approved. 'Excellent idea. It's a clear day so we should have a good view from the top.'

Despite Callum's efforts to contribute to the bill, Christophe insisted that this was his treat. Leaving the tea room, Alice spotted a taxi stand but there were several people already waiting and not a taxi in sight.

'We're going to need two taxis,' she murmured.

'Nah, we'll take the Métro,' Jack said. 'There's a stop just up the street.'

'But I cannot, in my shoes,' Nathalie protested. To the others, she explained, 'There are many stairs to climb in Métro.'

'How's she going to get up the Eiffel Tower?' Lara muttered.

Unfortunately, Alice hadn't been able to warn her about Nathalie's selective comprehension. The girl gave Lara an unpleasant smile which was more like a smirk.

'There is elevator.'

'Don't worry about your shoes,' Jack said. From the messenger bag that hung from his shoulder, he retrieved a pair of flat shoes. 'I figured you'd be ready for these by now.'

Nathalie looked at the ballerinas with contempt. 'They are not good with this skirt,' she said. Then she looked back up at Jack with a completely different expression. 'But how sweet that you think about me, *mon amour!*' She slipped off her heels and put on the flats.

Alice was struck with a sudden memory. How many years ago had it been? It was an early Saturday evening and they were going to the cinema. The weather was mild; it had been warm all day, and although her mother had urged her to take a cardigan, she hadn't wanted to cover up the new top she was wearing. When they emerged from the cinema, the temperature had dropped and she was cold. Jack had reached into his backpack and taken out a jumper.

'I got it from your mum,' he'd said. 'I knew you'd need it eventually.'

He hadn't changed at all, Alice thought. He was taking care of Nathalie, just like he'd taken care of her. She was suddenly aware of a lump in her throat, and she swallowed so hard she started coughing.

'Are you all right?' Callum asked, his eyes warm with concern.

She smiled brightly. 'Fine, I'm fine.' And she told herself that in the same circumstances, Callum would give her shoes, a sweater, anything that would make her more comfortable. He was just as caring, just as kind as Jack, and she was very, very lucky to have a man like that in her life. She swallowed again and the lump seemed to grow smaller. It didn't disappear though.

When they left the Métro, they encountered hordes of visitors armed with cameras and guidebooks, and they followed the crowds towards the Eiffel Tower. They couldn't all stay close together as they walked, so their

113

group split up. Nathalie and Claudine were walking between Callum and Harry, Lara talked with Christophe, and Alice unexpectedly found herself bringing up the rear with Jack. Quickly, she began to think of things they could talk about – his law course, her English degree, Paris versus London – but he spoke first.

'How do you like university?'

'Very much,' she replied. 'It's funny, I never thought of myself as an academic.'

'But you're a big reader,' he noted. 'You always had a book with you. I remember one of Lara's parties, when you disappeared. I found you in her bedroom, reading.'

She remembered that too. 'It was the last Harry Potter. I couldn't put it down.'

'Are you studying English at uni?'

'Yes. But what I really want to do is write. I think I'd like to be a journalist.' She smiled. 'I've always been curious about things. I could see myself becoming an investigative reporter.'

'Really?' Jack looked impressed. 'I don't remember you ever talking about a big career like that.'

'I've changed,' Alice said. She couldn't resist adding, 'Like you.'

'Me? Not so much, really.'

She wished she could say that the Jack she knew would never fall in love with a girl like Nathalie. But it would only sound like jealousy.

'Did I tell you, you look great?' he asked suddenly.

'Thanks, so do you,' she responded automatically.

'You haven't changed at all,' he said. 'I mean, you still look the same.'

She laughed lightly. 'Well, it's only been a couple of years. You don't look very different either. Maybe your hair's a bit longer.'

'Yeah, I need a haircut.'

'Oh, I think it looks nice like that.' Then, very quickly, she added, 'Of course, it doesn't matter what *I* think. Does Nathalie like your hair long?'

'I don't know,' he said. 'She's never said anything about it.'

She tried to think of some way to make that sound like a good thing. 'She's probably too in love with you to notice little things like hair.' Even as the words left her mouth she knew they sounded idiotic. And not very logical. Considering the attention Nathalie gave to every detail of her own appearance, surely she would notice everything about the way her husband-to-be looked.

But Jack didn't comment on it. He was looking straight ahead, at his fiancée some distance away. She had one hand on Harry's shoulder, balancing herself while she put her high-heeled shoes back on. She stumbled slightly, Harry steadied her, and she looked up at him with an expression that Alice thought was almost flirtatious. Or maybe that was how French girls acted with all men.

Claudine seemed to be flirting too. She had looped her arm through Harry's, and was chattering away non-stop. Alice recalled Claudine's comment in the tea room about needing an English boyfriend. It was a good thing Lara was walking ahead, talking with Christophe and not paying any attention.

'She's had a hard life,' Jack said suddenly. 'Nathalie. Her parents were killed in a car accident when she was very young, and she was taken in by distant relatives who weren't very kind. They're not even coming to the wedding. She's had to scrape to make her way in the world, all on her own.'

'That's rough,' Alice commented.

'I'm trying to make her happy,' he went on. 'It's not easy though. She wants a lot. I guess that's because she never had anything.'

She didn't know quite how to respond to that so she changed the subject. 'Lara says you want to move back to England after you graduate.'

He nodded. 'You know what I want to do? Don't laugh.'

'I won't,' she promised.

'I want to find a small town, like the one we grew up in, where I can be the local solicitor. Raise a family, get involved in the community . . .'

'Why would I laugh at that?' Alice asked.

'Because . . . I suppose because it doesn't sound very ambitious. Some of the guys I'm in lectures with, like Christophe, they've got big plans. They want to go the corporate route, make big deals, fly all over the world negotiating, that sort of thing.'

Alice tried to imagine Jack as a jet set legal eagle in a three-piece suit. It was impossible. 'That's not your thing.'

'No,' he agreed. 'I don't even want to make a lot of money. I just want to be comfortable, and . . . and happy.'

Alice spoke carefully. 'Is that what Nathalie wants too?'

He was silent for a minute. 'I don't know,' he said finally. 'We don't talk about the future much. Or . . .' He stopped suddenly, as if he was catching himself, as if he was afraid he was saying too much. Somehow, Alice knew what he'd been about to say: 'Or about anything else.' What kind of relationship did he and Nathalie really have? She shuddered.

He must have sensed it. 'Are you OK?' he asked.

'Fine, I'm fine.'

They were now in the queue to get inside the tower. Jack craned his neck to look up. Then he grinned.

'I know what's wrong. You're nervous about going up to the top. Remember the Ferris wheel?'

Alice closed her eyes. How could she have forgotten about that?

The fairground was a big one, with rides and games, musicians, clowns and acrobats. They'd spent a glorious day together, gorging on junk food, playing every silly game, driving bumper cars. Jack had won her that teddy bear shooting plastic ducks.

He wanted to ride the Ferris wheel, but Alice wasn't so keen. She'd always had a mild fear of heights. But he talked her into it and, just as the sun was setting, they bought their tickets and went into the little enclosed carriage, just the two of them. The wheel moved slowly and, as they rose, Alice was pleased to realize she could keep her fear under control. They talked, and laughed, and admired the view.

But then, when their carriage was at the very top, the wheel stopped. Was it supposed to do that, or was something wrong? They hung suspended in the air, and the carriage was rocking. That was when *she* started to shake, and she could feel the panic rising. She couldn't speak, she couldn't even breathe.

Immediately, Jack unbuckled his safety belt and moved to her side. He wrapped her in his arms and held her tightly. 'It's all right, everything's going to be OK,' he assured her softly. 'I'm here.' And he didn't let go.

Slowly, the panic began to seep away. She felt safe in his arms . . . more than safe. She felt like she could stay there for ever.

She could remember raising her face to look at him, to tell him she was better, but she had no opportunity to speak. He pressed his lips against hers, and they kissed. It went on and on, and it could have gone on for ever as far as she was concerned. The wheel finally started to move again, and she didn't even notice. That kiss, their first kiss . . . It carried a bolt of electricity. And with every kiss he gave her from that day on, she felt it.

Now, as they inched closer to the Eiffel Tower, her eyes were burning fiercely. She looked away and tried to keep her voice steady. 'How tall is it?'

'Over a thousand feet,' Jack said.

'It's OK. I'm not afraid of heights any more.' She waited a few seconds, to make sure her eyes wouldn't betray her feelings, before turning back to him. Then she caught her breath – because for one brief moment she could have sworn there was something in *his* eyes.

And then there was a big surge in the queue, a movement forwards, and within seconds they were on the lift. She was grateful that the crush of people in the car had separated them, but her heart was pounding so hard she feared he had heard it. And it had nothing to do with the lift. It was something else, something much deeper, something she shouldn't even allow herself to think about.

This couldn't be happening, she thought wildly. She wouldn't let it happen! She looked around for Cal, and kept her eyes firmly on him.

When the doors opened at the top, she allowed the crowd to push her out, and quickly searched for the others. She found them at the railing, gazing out over the famous view from the global icon. She waved and smiled, and hurried to join them.

'Isn't it amazing!' Lara exclaimed.

'Brilliant, just brilliant,' Alice said. She clutched Callum's arm. 'Did you bring your camera?'

'Yeah, it's right here,' he said, taking it out of his pocket.

She thrust it at Lara. 'Take a picture of Cal and me, please.'

She snuggled close to him, and he put his arm around her. As soon as Lara finished, she took the camera back.

'Now a picture of the bride and groom!'

Nathalie wasn't enthusiastic. 'That is a tourist thing.'

'I don't care, it's important. Really. You'll thank me for it later.' Alice knew she was babbling, but she couldn't stop. 'It will be romantic. Jack, Nathalie, stand over there.'

The couple obliged. Nathalie's expression was blank, and Jack looked oddly tense.

'Put your arm round her, Jack,' Alice urged. To her own ears, her voice sounded shrill, but no one else seemed to notice.

Jack put his arm around Nathalie, and Nathalie inched closer to him.

Alice held the camera to her eyes. 'Now, smile,' she said, and clicked.

'Shall I take another?' she asked, lowering the camera. But now, everyone had turned away to look at the view. It was too bad, in a way. She didn't think the photo would turn out very well. Her hands had been shaking.

Chapter Nine

Back on the Métro there were no seats, so they stood close together and clutched a bar for support. Harry was in high spirits.

'I've got a little story about the Eiffel Tower that I'll bet even you locals don't know,' he announced.

Lara wasn't surprised. Harry was a master of trivia; he had a treasure trove of anecdotes and he was always coming up with odd little stories he'd collected. Sometimes they were amusing, but at other times they were just bizarre, even outrageous. Lara listened with some trepidation as he launched into this one.

'There's this American woman, her name was Erika Something, who was totally obsessed with the Eiffel Tower. So she organized a ceremony, on the top of the tower, and married it, in 2007. Now she calls herself Erika Eiffel. It's a true story, I swear. She's been on the telly talking about it.'

Lara checked to see their companions' reactions to this bit of weirdness. Claudine was giggling hysterically. Callum, so accustomed to these stories, grinned and rolled his eyes. Nathalie either didn't understand or wasn't interested and neither Jack nor Alice were paying much attention – they both seemed to be daydreaming. Christophe, however, was clearly puzzled.

'This is not possible,' he said. 'One cannot legally marry a thing.'

'She called it a "commitment ceremony",' Harry told him.

Christophe was still perplexed. 'Even so . . . what kind of a woman would want to marry an inanimate object?'

Harry grinned. 'Well, you have to admit, the Eiffel Tower has a certain masculine quality, if you get my meaning.'

Callum chuckled, but Lara groaned. She was used to Harry's puerile sense of humour and she just wrote it off as a boy thing. This was only a mildly risqué remark, but even so, she didn't miss the flash of distaste that crossed Christophe's face. She couldn't help feeling a little embarrassed. Couldn't Harry understand that his jokes weren't always appropriate?

When they left the Métro, she hung back to speak to

Alice. 'Can you believe Harry? He can be so adolescent sometimes.'

Alice looked at her blankly. 'What are you talking about?'

'That remark he just made, about the Eiffel Tower.'

'I didn't hear it,' Alice said.

Lara's brow furrowed. 'Are you OK? You seem a bit out of it.'

'I'm just tired, I think.'

'Well, wake up,' Lara ordered her. 'We're going to a posh dinner, remember?'

Alice smiled. 'I'll be fine.'

It was a short walk to the Pompidou Centre. Christophe announced that it was one of his favourite buildings in Paris.

'It was quite controversial when it opened in the nineteen seventies,' he told them. 'Some people felt that such a modern, high-tech building was out of place in Paris. But I think it blends in beautifully with traditional Parisian architecture.'

'I think so too,' Lara declared with more enthusiasm than she actually felt. Actually, she thought the place was very peculiar, with all the brightly coloured tubes running alongside the building. Christophe explained them.

'The architect placed the inner structures on the outside,' he pointed out. 'The tubes contain the plumbing, electricity, all the elements that are usually hidden. Very original, yes?'

Harry shrugged. 'If you say so. Looks kind of weird to me. Where's the restaurant?'

Lara winced. Couldn't he at least pretend to have some interest? Fake a bit of sophistication?

They were an hour early for dinner so Jack suggested a walk around. They didn't have to go far for entertainment – just on the other side of the Pompidou Centre was a huge plaza that beckoned with all kinds of activities.

A woman squatting on the ground was playing some exotic, Asian harp-like instrument. A circle of people had gathered around a man who was juggling a dozen red balls. Another man, dressed as a clown, twisted balloons into animal shapes. There were artists who coaxed passers-by into having portraits and caricatures done, a mime performer, and costumed people posing as statues. A woman had set up a mini-salon where she offered to weave feathers and coloured threads in people's hair.

Flocks of tourists mingled with locals who headed towards the cafés that faced the plaza. A group of young boys were kicking a football. Lara and the others wandered around, taking in the scene, and then paused next to an elderly man who had started playing an accordion. Normally, Lara thought of the accordion as a rather hackneyed and old-fashioned instrument, but in this man's hands the sounds that emerged were sweet and rhythmic. Other people came round, some to drop a coin or two in the paper cup that rested by the man's side, but most stuck around to listen.

The accordionist struck up a tune that Lara recognized. It was one of her favourites: Édith Piaf's 'La Vie En Rose'. She hummed along. Other spectators were getting into it too, and one young couple joined hands. The girl put her other hand on his shoulder, he put his on her waist and they started to dance. Another couple began dancing, and then another. Some total stranger approached Claudine, and seconds later they were dancing too.

No one was laughing at them or gawking – it seemed perfectly natural, under the setting sun of Paris, to dance outside amidst onlookers and jugglers and clowns. It was absolutely enchanting, and Lara wanted to be part of it. She took Harry's hand.

'C'mon, let's dance!'

Harry made a face.

'Are you crazy? In front of all these people?'

She wasn't only disappointed, she was annoyed. Harry was perfectly willing to tell stupid jokes in front of people he barely knew but he wouldn't dance in public.

'May I have this dance?'

She turned to see Christophe extending his arms towards her. Quickly, she handed her bags to Alice and shot a triumphant glance at Harry.

Christophe had no problem with dancing in public, and for good reason – he was an excellent dancer. He moved smoothly and gracefully, leading her lightly but with just enough pressure so that she could follow easily. As he twirled her, she glanced at Harry to see if he was watching.

But Harry had hooked up with the kids playing football and wasn't paying any attention to her at all. Here she was, under Paris skies, in the arms of a handsome Frenchman, dancing to an accordionist playing a romantic French song – and Harry didn't care! He wasn't even remotely interested, forget about being jealous!

What did she have to do to get some kind of reaction from him? She let her hand move very slowly across Christophe's shoulder blades till she was touching his neck. Christophe responded by pulling her closer, until her head was resting on his chest. Closing her eyes, she visualized Harry seeing this, rushing towards them, stopping the dance and ordering Christophe to take his hands off his girlfriend.

But Harry would never do anything like that; it wasn't his style. She should know this by now; she should be used to his ways. So why was she feeling so dissatisfied?

The music stopped, the accordionist began another, livelier song, and Jack announced that it was time to go up to the restaurant. They all went down the sloping plaza to a special door with a sign that said 'Restaurant George', where a uniformed man ushered them into a lift.

When they got out, they were at the top of the building and just outside the doors that led into the restaurant.

'I want to change my dress,' Lara told Alice. 'Come with me?'

They told the others they'd meet them inside and headed off in search of the ladies. It was a spacious, modern room, and – fortunately – empty. Alice took Lara's purchase out of the bag while Lara started unbuttoning her shirt dress.

'Christophe's quite a dancer,' Alice commented as she took the price tag off the dress. 'You two looked really nice together.'

'I'm glad *someone* noticed,' Lara declared.

'What do you mean?'

'Harry certainly didn't care. I mean, really, Alice, there I was with another man's hands all over me, and he didn't bat an eyelid!'

'Harry's not the jealous type,' said Alice.

'No. But maybe he needs to be.'

'Lara! Are you saying you're actually interested in Christophe?'

Lara slipped off her dress. 'Who wouldn't be? I mean, look at him! He's gorgeous, he's charming, he's got beautiful manners – he's got class! Something Harry is seriously lacking in.'

'But that's never bothered you before,' Alice protested. 'And you barely know Christophe.'

'Look, I'm not saying I'm ready to dump Harry for Christophe. But I certainly wouldn't mind if Harry thought he had competition. If he thinks Christophe is into me, maybe he'll clean up his act and start appreciating me.'

'Harry appreciates you, Lara,' Alice insisted.

'Not like Callum appreciates you,' Lara grumbled.

Something in Alice's expression changed, and Lara gazed at her curiously. 'What's the matter?'

'Nothing.'

'That's what you keep saying, but something's going on in your head. And don't tell me you're just tired, I don't believe that. Did you have a fight with Cal?' She answered her own question. 'No, you never fight with Cal.'

'Never,' Alice echoed. 'Cal's perfect.'

'Yes, absolutely perfect,' Lara agreed. 'Too bad you're not in love with him.'

'Well, not *yet*,' Alice said. 'Give me time.'

Lara shook her head. 'Time won't make any difference.'

'Why do you say that?' Alice asked sharply.

'You're never going to fall in love with Cal. Not as long as you're still in love with Jack.'

Alice's shoulders slumped.

'I'm right, aren't I?'

For a moment, Alice didn't speak. She stared at her reflection in the mirror as if she was searching for an answer. Then, finally, she nodded.

'I thought I was over it. I honestly believed all I felt towards him was anger. But today, talking, remembering . . . Oh, Lara, I don't think I've ever stopped loving him.'

Lara's heart was full, and it ached for her best friend. Alice had managed to hide her feelings for so long. Two years ago Lara had listened to her cry, and comforted her. Then Alice stopped talking about Jack and she seemed fine. Maybe she really *was* fine. Then Lara had to go and drag her to this wedding and bring it all back. She was a rotten best friend.

'I'm sorry,' she said.

'For what?'

'For making you come to this wedding. For bringing it all back.'

Alice smiled wanly. 'It's not your fault. I wanted to come, I wanted reassurance that I didn't love him any more. But that's not what I'm getting, is it?'

'What are you going to do?'

'What *can* I do? He's getting married the day after tomorrow!'

'He's not married yet,' Lara said.

'He's getting married,' Alice repeated. 'And I don't want to talk about this now. Turn around, I'll zip you up. This dress is really lovely, Lara.'

Lara gave up – for the time being. She turned to the mirror and admired her reflection. 'OK, let's go. I want to see if Harry even notices that I've changed my clothes.'

They went into the restaurant and looked around. Lara was too distracted by the decor to search for their companions. It was a very cool place, unlike any restaurant she'd seen before. Metal sculptures, blue pipes, crisp white tables and chairs, with a vase containing a single red rose on each table. A beautiful woman, all in black, came towards them. She looked more like a model than a waitress, and all of a sudden Lara felt a lot less French.

Alice gave her Jack's name but the waitress simply raised her perfectly arched eyebrows. Then Lara remembered who was paying for this weekend.

'De Trouville?' she asked.

The woman's face cleared, and she nodded respectfully. In French, she said something that Lara assumed meant 'follow me', and led them out on to the terrace. They spotted the others standing around a table in the centre. Alice started towards them, but before Lara had gone more than two steps Christophe broke away from the group and came to her.

'*Ah, tu est trop belle ce soir, Lara!*'

She wanted to hear it again, so she faked a puzzled look.

'You are so beautiful tonight,' he repeated.

With his accent, the compliment sounded even better in English. '*Merci beaucoup,*' she replied with a smile.

He put a light hand on her upper arm and escorted her to the group. Even though it had been at least a dozen years since she'd last seen her, Lara recognized

Jack's mother. The elegant woman seemed not to have aged at all, and she still wore her jet-black hair pulled back in a tight chignon. She was clearly doing well from her marriage – she wore a dress that could have been in the window of any of those shops on rue de Faubourg Saint-Honoré. And her black quilted handbag with the chain strap bore those famous overlapping Cs of Chanel.

She was standing by her son, and Jack beckoned for Lara to join them.

'Mother, you remember cousin Lara,' he said.

The woman turned frigidly cold blue eyes towards her. There was no sign of recognition on her face – in fact, there wasn't any expression at all. Lara figured this was probably due to a certain type of injection that wouldn't allow much in the way of a facial reaction. There wasn't a line on her face and her complexion was flawless.

'*Bonsoir*, Lara,' she murmured, and leaned forward so they could kiss the air near each of their cheeks. Fortunately, she then switched to English. 'May I present my husband, Jean-Louis de Trouville.'

They made a seriously odd couple – he had to be at least thirty years older than his artificially rejuvenated wife. Lara managed a weak '*Enchanté, monsieur*' as the positively ancient man bowed slightly in her direction, and then turned away as if she didn't merit any more attention.

A waiter approached carrying a tray laden with glasses, and addressed Madame de Trouville first. 'Champagne, madame?' He made his way to each of the women before offering drinks to the men. Jack and Christophe each accepted a glass with a *merci* but Harry shook his head.

'Can I have a beer instead?'

Lara fervently wished for a hole to suddenly appear beneath her so she could sink inside it. Beside her, Christophe uttered a soft chuckle.

'He is very English, your boyfriend.'

Jack slapped Harry on the back with a laugh. 'I could go for a lager myself right now,' he said. 'But take a champagne; I think there's going to be a toast.'

Sure enough, Monsieur de Trouville raised his glass. He spoke in a monotonous manner but he enunciated clearly. He didn't sound particularly enthusiastic about it, but Lara was pleased she could understand that he was wishing health and happiness to the bride and groom. Her school French was actually coming back to her.

Despite the lack of emotion in his tone, Nathalie beamed happily. Her arm was linked with Jack's but her eyes were on the old man. *Of course*, Lara thought. *That was where the money would come from*. She could practically see those red-soled shoes dancing in Nathalie's head.

It was all becoming clear to her now. Monsieur de Trouville was not only very rich, he was very old. Money would be coming, and it might not be that long from now. Of course, Jack's mother would inherit de Trouville's money, but Nathalie would assume she'd continue to be generous with her son.

Jack's mother was standing by her side now, and Lara felt like she had to make some effort at conversation.

'That was a lovely toast,' she said.

Madame de Trouville responded with that same peculiar puckered-lip expression that Nathalie often made – the one that seemed to say, 'OK, whatever.' Did all French women do this?

Lara tried another conversation starter. 'Jack told us you are giving him and Nathalie this wedding. That's very generous of you.'

This time the woman actually responded with words. 'It was not easy to convince my husband. He has three grown children from a previous marriage, and none of them have jobs. He supports them all. And of course, we have a lifestyle to maintain.' She sighed. '*C'est la vie*. But my poor Jack. I am afraid he will not benefit from my marriage.'

Interesting, Lara thought. She wondered if Nathalie knew that Jack wasn't in line for some great inheritance. She made her way over to Harry. As she'd expected, he didn't even notice that she was wearing a new dress. He was too busy studying his champagne glass.

'I don't understand why this stuff is so expensive,' he said. 'It doesn't taste like much.'

'That's because it requires a refined palate,' Lara replied. '*I* think it's delicious.'

The waiter came by again. This time he held a plate of exquisite little nibbly things.

Harry looked at them suspiciously. 'What are those?'

'*Escargots en croûte*,' the waiter replied.

'Huh?'

Lara translated. 'Snails in puff pastry.'

Harry stepped back in horror, as if he expected to be attacked by the canapés. Lara shook her head wearily.

'I'm going to look at the view,' she announced. 'Want to come?'

'No thanks. I'm going to see if I can order a beer,' Harry said.

Lara turned away and crossed the terrace in the direction of the windows. When she got to the other side, she saw Christophe and Nathalie talking. And from their expressions, she could see that they weren't just making polite conversation. They both looked tense, and Nathalie was smoking.

She couldn't be pregnant, Lara thought. Every woman she'd ever known who smoked had quit when they got pregnant. Her own older sister, a chain smoker, had given it up. Even a woman who thought only of herself wouldn't put an unborn child at risk.

So Nathalie was marrying Jack because she thought he had money, Lara decided. But why was Jack marrying her?

They didn't see her approaching, and she strained to hear what they were talking about. Of course, it was all in French, and very fast French at that. But she did manage to catch a few words from Nathalie. Something like '*Je raconterai à tout le monde la vérité sur toi.*'

She searched her memory for definitions. *La vérité* . . . that meant the truth. The truth of you? The truth *about* you? *Raconter* . . . to tell. *Tout le monde*, that meant everyone. I'll tell everyone the truth about you? It sounded like a threat.

Then Nathalie saw her, and stopped speaking. She walked away from Christophe without saying goodbye, and passed Lara without a greeting either.

'What was that all about?' Lara asked Christophe. 'She didn't look very happy.'

Christophe shrugged. 'It was nothing. Come, see the view.' He took her arm, and once again she marvelled at how lovely it felt to be treated like a lady. They crossed the terrace to face the windows. There, she gazed out over a panorama of Paris that absolutely took her breath away. The Eiffel Tower may have been a lot higher, but this view was much more appealing. Paris as seen from the tower was interesting. This view was something else. Everything was closer and you could see all the lovely details of the rooftops and chimneys. It stirred her heart.

Another couple, not from their party, came over to the windows. Hand in hand, they stood there quietly, not noticing Lara and Christophe. She could see why. From the way they were looking at each other, she knew they were in love. And something she couldn't put into words filled her senses.

She didn't have to say a word – Christophe seemed to know exactly what she was feeling. He spoke softly, as if he didn't want to disturb the mood.

'Poets say it is the most beautiful city in the world. And of course, the most romantic. Why else would so many great love stories be set here? Have you ever seen *Casablanca*, Lara?'

She had, actually, on TV late one night, a long time ago. It was an old film, in black and white. Humphrey Bogart and Ingrid Bergman played star-crossed lovers during the Second World War.

'Doesn't it take place in Morocco?' she asked.

'Yes. But do you remember where they meet and fall in love? And what he says to her at the end, when they are about to separate and they know they will never see each other again? "We'll always have Paris".'

It came back to her. 'Yes. I remember that.'

'If you fall in love in Paris, that love can never die. You see, Lara, one may love to live in other cities, but in Paris, we live to love.'

He spoke like a poet. Lara saw the couple standing by the windows at the other end of the terrace. As she watched, the man gently took the woman in his arms and kissed her. And now she knew what she was feeling – a sense of longing and envy. She wanted to be kissed like that. In Paris.

That was when she became aware of Christophe's arm. It was round her shoulders. She caught her breath and looked up at him. He looked down at her, with eyes so soft, so warm. Never in her life had she been with a man who looked at her so tenderly . . . his grip on her shoulder tightened and she didn't resist.

From just behind them was the sound of a cough, a loud one. Lara pulled away from Christophe and turned. Callum was standing there.

'Um . . . we're going into dinner now.'

'Great, brilliant, I'm starving,' Lara exclaimed just a little too brightly. With her heart pounding and her head spinning, she left Christophe's side and hurried past Callum.

Chapter Ten

Jack's mother had made a seating plan and Alice waited by the long table to see where she would be placed. Lara, looking oddly flushed, arrived at the table, followed by Callum and Christophe. Madame de Trouville looked at Callum and raised her eyebrows.

'Yes?'

'Oh, I'm sorry!' Alice exclaimed. 'I don't think you were introduced on the terrace. Callum, this is Jack's mother, Madame de Trouville. Madame, this is Callum Greene.' She took a deep breath, and added, 'My boyfriend.'

There, she'd said it. She'd managed to get the word out. It was ironic in a way – after all, she'd just confessed to Lara how she felt about Jack. But she needed to say it, to remind herself that this was now, not then. Callum must have heard her. He looked at her and smiled. She

141

was pleased to see him look so happy. But really it was far too late. She felt tainted by a strong feeling of guilt.

Alice was directed to a seat at one end, and the waiter standing by pulled out the chair for her. Callum was placed next to her. Jack's stepfather was at the head of the table, just by Alice. Alice gave him a polite smile and drummed up the beginnings of some small talk.

'This is a lovely restaurant,' she said.

He gave her a brief, dismissive glance and said nothing. Madame de Trouville, sitting on his other side, explained.

'My husband doesn't speak English.'

She didn't bother to translate what Alice had said for him, and he didn't seem to care. Alice was actually relieved that she wouldn't have to attempt any further communication with the haughty-looking man. She'd rather hoped that Jack and Nathalie would be on her side of the table so she wouldn't have to look at them during the meal. But they'd been placed almost opposite her, directly in her line of view. Every time she looked up, she'd be looking at Jack.

She wasn't really much of a drinker, but she wasn't unhappy when new glasses of champagne appeared. From the other end of the table, Christophe got up, and Alice didn't miss the wariness on Nathalie's face.

Remembering Christophe's faux pas in the tea room, when he'd mentioned her parents, Alice couldn't blame her.

Raising his glass, Christophe spoke first in French, and then in English.

'To our hosts, Monsieur and Madame de Trouville,' he said. 'And to Jack and Nathalie. Two couples who exemplify the spirit of true love.'

He was looking more at Nathalie than at Jack as he spoke. Nathalie allowed him a small nod and a satisfied smile. It was a strange toast, Alice thought. Surely if Christophe and Jack were as close as they seemed to be, Christophe would know that Jack's mother's marriage wasn't exactly a love match. You could just look at them and know the story – she wanted his money, he wanted a trophy wife, someone attractive and younger.

Maybe Christophe was being sarcastic. Maybe it was a private joke between him and Jack. But putting Jack and Nathalie in the same category meant only one thing to Alice: Christophe knew they weren't in love either.

She gazed across the table at Jack, to assess his reaction to the toast. Faint lines had appeared between his eyes and another flash of memory jolted her. She knew that expression. She used to see it whenever he had to visit his mother. The only word she could think of to describe it was . . . wistful. Maybe forlorn. It wasn't the kind of look you expected to see on the face of someone who was getting married.

Their eyes met – and she quickly averted hers. Turning to Callum, she said, 'Can you believe the waitresses here? They all look like supermodels!'

Callum smiled. 'Why would I notice them when I'm with the most beautiful girl in the restaurant?'

She smiled back at him. This was the kind of thing a guy in love would say. And Lara's words came floating back: 'You're never going to fall in love with Cal. Not as long as you're still in love with Jack.'

It was true. And she didn't know how she was going to deal with it. She couldn't have Jack. Was it fair to let Callum go on thinking he was number one in her heart?

'Are you OK?' Callum asked her.

'Yes, of course. Why?'

'You look like something's bothering you.'

'I'm just hungry,' she lied. 'Oh look, here comes the food.'

Callum continued to look at her with concern, but the arrival of the first course distracted him.

The menu had been selected by Jack's mother and she didn't appear to have spared any expense. The starter was a delicate cold asparagus soup. As a waiter poured a bit of wine into Monsieur de Trouville's glass to try, she heard Harry joke 'Is that all he's giving the poor guy?' and she could sense Lara cringing. Monsieur de Trouville looked at the wine as if he was examining it, twirled the glass, then held it to his nose and sniffed deeply. Finally he took a sip, gazed up at the sky as if pondering the taste and nodded to the waiter. Everyone's glasses were filled.

Jack's mother spoke to no one in particular. 'What did you young people do today?'

Nathalie responded in rapid French. Jack touched her arm.

'In English, Nathalie. Our guests don't speak French.'

'But your father, he does not know English,' Nathalie protested.

Jack lowered his voice. '*Step*father, Nathalie. Don't worry about him, he's not interested in what we did today. And you need to practise your English.'

Nathalie pouted for a second, then spoke sweetly. 'As you wish, *chéri*.' She turned back to Madame de Trouville. 'We shop.'

'And we went to the Eiffel Tower,' Jack reminded her.

'*Oui*,' Nathalie said. Then she dramatically clapped her hand to her mouth. 'Oh, I am so sorry, *mon amour*! I mean, yes. Please, I beg of you, forgive me.' Claudine started to giggle, and Nathalie did too.

The waiter came and collected the bowls.

'What are your plans for tomorrow?' Jack's mother asked.

'I was thinking about taking everyone to Montmartre,' Jack said.

'But, Jack, you must have things to do,' Callum said. 'You shouldn't have to show tourists round on the day before your wedding. We can take care of ourselves.'

Madame de Trouville answered for him. 'He has nothing to do. I'm making all the arrangements.'

'Oh, *maman*, you are so kind!' Nathalie gushed. 'May I call you *maman*?' Her voice became sorrowful. 'I have no *maman* of my own.'

'Of course, my dear,' the woman said, patting her arm.

'My father and a couple of other relatives are arriving tomorrow evening,' Jack told Callum. 'The other guests don't arrive till Sunday. And I'm already packed for the . . . the honeymoon.' He seemed to be having a hard time with the word.

'Where are you going?' Alice asked politely.

'The Riviera,' Jack told her. 'I wanted to take Nathalie to the Cotswolds but she prefers the beach.'

'Well, you'll have time to visit the Cotswolds when you move back to England,' Callum said.

'Cotswolds,' Nathalie repeated. 'It is chic?'

'It's very pretty,' Alice told her.

Nathalie responded with pursed lips.

'So we'll all go to Montmartre tomorrow,' Jack declared.

'But I must find a tiara tomorrow,' Nathalie protested. 'I do not think there is nice shop for tiara in Montmartre. There is only cheap souvenir shop in Montmartre.'

Jack briefly closed his eyes and for a moment Alice thought he was in pain.

The waiter returned and began putting down plates of duck breast with a fragrant sauce. The diners attacked it gratefully – partly, Alice suspected, because it provided an excuse not to make conversation. People ate steadily and silently.

But Nathalie still had her mind on her headpiece. 'I think Galeries Lafayette may be good place to find tiara,' she said.

Jack sighed. 'Nathalie, do you really need a tiara?'

'*Oui, mon amour*,' Nathalie said firmly. 'This is my wedding. I must be perfect.'

Callum spoke gallantly. 'I'm sure you'll look lovely in anything you wear.'

Nathalie sniffed. 'A bride must have a tiara.'

'I have a tiara,' Madame de Trouville announced. 'I

will lend it to you for your wedding.'

Jack looked relieved, but Nathalie's lower lip jutted out.

'I want my own tiara,' she declared.

Jack cast a desperate look at Alice, and Alice couldn't resist intervening to help out.

'You know, Nathalie, in England, whenever a member of the royal family marries, the Queen lends the bride one of her tiaras.'

'That's right,' Lara piped up. 'I read that she lent one to Kate Middleton.'

Jack was nodding too. 'So you'd be respecting an English tradition if you accept the loan of a tiara from your mother-in-law, Nathalie.'

Nathalie didn't seem very happy about this, but she gave in. '*D'accord*,' she said to Jack's mother. 'I accept your tiara.'

Jack looked at Alice and mouthed the words 'thank you'.

'You're welcome,' she mouthed back.

They both smiled. Then, as if they'd done something terrible, they both looked away.

After the waiter took the orders for dessert, Nathalie rose.

'*Excusez-moi*,' she said. Taking her handbag, she left the table.

Claudine got up. 'Me too,' she said, and hurried after Nathalie.

Jack shook his head. 'They're going out to have a cigarette. She thinks I don't know she smokes but I can smell it on her.'

'It's not good for her,' Alice commented.

'I know. Especially—' He stopped suddenly.

'In her condition?' Alice asked softly.

Jack nodded.

The waiter placed a *crème caramel* in front of her, but Alice didn't pick up her spoon. She'd just lost her appetite.

Chapter Eleven

'Well, at least now we know why he's marrying her,' Lara declared. 'I was right. I knew he couldn't love her.'

'They slept together,' Alice replied. 'They must have had some kind of feeling for each other.'

'Men will sleep with women they don't love,' Lara declared.

Alice couldn't argue with that, mainly because her mouth was now full of toothpaste. They were standing side by side at the sinks in the bathroom the next morning, and Lara hadn't stopped talking since they'd woken up.

'She probably seduced him. I mean, Jack's a good person, but he's still a man. She's marrying him because she wants her baby to have a father, and he's marrying her to do the right thing. But there's no way they're in love, Alice.'

Alice spat out the toothpaste. 'Maybe not. But it doesn't change anything.'

'You have to be hurting,' Lara said.

Alice nodded. 'I didn't want to admit it, not even to myself. But in the back of my mind, there was a little fantasy going on.'

'That Jack would realize he still loved you and he'd stop the wedding?'

'Something like that.' Alice took out a brush and started working on her hair, furiously, so that it almost hurt. As if physical pain might cancel out some of the emotional pain.

'It's all so *wrong*!' Lara cried hotly. 'I'll bet she wanted to get pregnant so he'd have to marry her. She thinks he's got money, that they're going to live in a stately home, keep a flat in Paris, and she's going to have a million red-soled shoes. What she doesn't know is that Jack will not be getting any money from his stepfather. According to Jack's mother, it's all going to his three kids from a previous marriage.' She sighed. 'Too bad it's not just about that now.'

'I know,' Alice said. She took out a mascara wand. 'Because if Jack found out Nathalie was marrying him for money, he'd break it off. And if Nathalie found out he didn't have any, *she'd* break it off.' She smiled sadly.

'That was part of my fantasy. But even if they learn about each other before the wedding, it won't make any difference. There's no way Jack wouldn't marry her now. Not when she's going to have his baby. You know how old-fashioned he is!' In her reflection, she watched a stream of black mascara rolling down her face.

Silently, Lara handed her a tissue, and she mopped her eyes. 'I don't know if I'm crying for me or him. Think about what his life's going to be like, Lara. They get married, she realizes he's not rich. She has the baby, and then she finds some poor idiot who has a few quid in the bank and she's out of there, taking the kid with her. Can you imagine what that's going to do to him?'

'It'll break his heart,' Lara said.

'It's ironic,' Alice mused. 'Two days ago, if I'd thought of this scenario, I would have said it served him right after what he did to me. But now—'

She was interrupted by a drumming on the bathroom door. 'Hey, have you girls drowned in the toilet or something?' Harry yelled.

'We're coming,' Alice called back. To Lara, she asked, 'Where are we going today – Montmartre?'

'You are. I'm not going with you,' Lara told her.

'You're not? How come?'

'Well, there are relatives arriving today. Aunt Sylvia

and Uncle Ronald. And Jack's father, of course.'

'Jack said they're not coming till tonight.'

'I think it's more like late afternoon. I need to hang around here and greet them.'

Alice was surprised. 'Why? I've never even heard you mention Aunt Sylvia and Uncle Ronald. And you're not close to Jack's father.'

Lara suddenly seemed very interested in applying lip liner. It took her a while before she responded. 'It just seems like the right thing to do. And Mum will want a report on them since she couldn't come.'

Alice had a sudden suspicion. 'Is Christophe coming to Montmartre with us?' she asked.

Lara wouldn't meet her eyes. 'No. He doesn't like Montmartre. He says it's too touristy.'

'Lara! You're staying here so you can hang out with Christophe!'

Lara finally faced her. 'OK, maybe I am. So what?'

Alice gave her a reproving look. 'So maybe Harry is going to be very, very hurt.'

'Huh.' Lara gathered up her things and tossed them back into her wash bag. 'And maybe Harry won't even notice that I'm not there.' She started towards the door.

'Wait a minute,' Alice said, looking at her friend suspiciously. 'You're not planning to take Claudine's advice on how to improve your language skills, are you?'

Lara seemed to be having some difficulty meeting her eyes. 'I don't know what you're talking about,' she said at last. And with that, she left.

Alice went back to work on her own make-up. She didn't want to think that Lara was seriously interested in Christophe. She felt reasonably sure that Lara was just enjoying flirting with a handsome stranger in the hope that Harry might notice another man paying attention to her. But Alice was going to have to keep an eye on her. Lara was impetuous at times and she didn't always think about the consequences of her actions. And her concern for Lara and Harry just might keep her from brooding about other relationships. Like Nathalie and Jack. Like herself and Callum.

She returned to the bedroom. Harry and Lara had already left, but Callum was waiting for her.

'What's up with Lara?'

'I don't know. Why are you asking?'

'She was really twitchy about something,' he said.

Alice felt a rush of affection for him. It was so typically Cal, to be able to read someone's mood and care if that mood seemed a bit off. But given the fact that Callum was Harry's best friend, she didn't want to mention Lara's ongoing efforts to make Harry jealous.

'Oh, she's worried about Jack.'

'Why?'

'She thinks he's only marrying Nathalie because she's pregnant, that he doesn't really love her. And she thinks Nathalie's only marrying Jack because she thinks he's going to inherit money.'

'What do *you* think?' He opened the door for her.

'*I* think it's none of our business,' she said, walking out into the corridor.

'But he's your friend,' Callum remarked. 'You care about him, don't you?'

She looked at him. It was a normal question, given the conversation. And yet, behind his searching eyes, she sensed a bigger question.

'Of course, but there's nothing I can do,' she said finally. Looking away, she added, 'I really don't want to think about it. I want us to enjoy ourselves.'

She knew it wasn't a very satisfying response, but she couldn't think of anything else to say. Hopefully, once they were in the dining room there would be other conversations they could join.

But that wasn't to be. Christophe sat with Claudine, who was talking non-stop in French. Christophe nodded occasionally, but looked exceedingly bored. Jack and Nathalie seemed to be in the midst of a tense discussion. Alice couldn't hear what they were talking about, but their expressions made it clear that something was going on. Harry and Lara were together, but Alice saw they didn't look too happy either.

'I have to stay and see the relatives,' Lara was saying.

'Then I'll stay too,' Harry told her.

'Don't be silly, you'll be bored stiff. Just go with the others and see more of Paris.'

'But I *want* to stay.'

Lara looked surprised. 'You do?'

Harry gave her an abashed grin. 'Actually, to tell the truth . . . I found a TV room here, and the football's on this afternoon. You know I'm not big on sightseeing. I could hang around here, meet your relatives, watch the game . . .'

Obviously he couldn't see Lara's face fall the way Alice could. *Wrong answer, Harry,* she thought sadly. She turned to Callum.

'Let's get breakfast.'

As they looked over the buffet, Callum glanced back at the two less-than-happy couples. 'I'm getting some strange vibes here.'

'What do you mean?'

'It just doesn't feel like a wedding weekend.'

Alice knew what he meant. She'd been to weddings

before, and he probably had too. Usually, there was exhilaration in the air, a giddy feeling, lots of laughter and happily frantic activity, a sense of anticipation and excitement. But the tone was usually set by the bride and groom, and neither Nathalie nor Jack seemed caught up in the event at all.

'It *is* a bit glum,' Alice agreed. 'But, like I said, Lara doesn't think it's a love match. I hope it's not too boring for you.'

'I'm OK,' he assured her. 'I just hope the general mood of the bride and groom isn't contagious.' He was looking at Lara and Harry as he spoke, but Alice had to wonder if he was thinking of another couple too.

'Let's just enjoy Paris today,' she said simply.

They picked up their food and headed back to the table. At that moment, Nathalie suddenly pushed back her chair and walked out of the room. Jack stared after her with a grim expression. Alice and Callum stood by him uncertainly.

'What's up?' Callum asked.

Jack sighed. 'I don't know what's the matter with her.'

'Maybe it's pre-wedding jitters,' Alice said.

'Maybe,' Jack echoed, but he didn't look convinced. He got up. 'I'm going to get my jacket,' he said and started out of the room. Looking back over his shoulder, he called, 'Whoever wants to go to Montmartre, meet out the front in ten minutes, OK?'

After breakfast, Alice ran back to the room for a jumper and then she went outside. Nathalie was there, sitting on a bench and talking on her mobile. Her voice was animated and she seemed to be arguing with the person on the other end of the line. Alice turned away politely, even though she couldn't understand the conversation.

Finally Nathalie yelled something into the phone, hit a button and put it down on the bench. Then she took out a cigarette, lit it and stared at Alice as if challenging her to say something.

The silence was deafening, and Alice searched her brain for a topic. 'Does Jack still collect comic books?' she asked.

Nathalie looked blank.

'You know, books with pictures and captions. When he was a teenager, he had a huge collection. Superman, Batman . . . that sort of thing. He even took them with him to university.'

Nathalie shrugged. 'I never see comic books.'

'Does he collect something else now?'

'I don't know.' And from her expression, Alice could see that she didn't care either.

Claudine came outside and lit a cigarette. Nathalie began talking to her in French, glancing every now and then at Alice, as if to make sure Alice couldn't understand. Then she put out her cigarette and went back inside.

Claudine turned to Alice. 'You come shopping with us?'

'I thought we were going to Montmartre.'

Claudine made a face. 'Montmartre, it is for tourists.'

Alice smiled. 'We *are* tourists.'

Claudine dropped her cigarette, crushed it with her foot and started back inside. As she walked in, Callum came out.

'How's the bride?' he asked Alice. 'Has she recovered from the jitters?'

'I'm not sure,' Alice said. 'I don't think she and Claudine are coming with us to Montmartre.'

Just then, a mobile rang. It was Nathalie's; she'd left it on the bench. Alice looked at it uncertainly.

'Should I answer it?' she wondered.

Callum shook his head. 'Best to let the person leave a message.' But looking at the phone, he frowned.

'That's strange. Didn't Jack say Nathalie's an orphan?'

'Yeah, why?'

'Well, the caller name on the screen is *Maman*.'

Nathalie came back out. 'I look for my mobile!'

159

'It's on the bench,' Alice told her. 'You had a phone call.'

A flash of alarm crossed Nathalie's face. 'You did not answer?'

Alice shook her head. And she didn't mention the name on the screen. Nathalie snatched up the phone, pressed a button and held it to her ear. Whatever message she got made her clench her teeth. She pressed in more numbers, and whoever she called got an angry response from her. Alice wished there was someone around who could at least give her a hint as to what this was all about. All Alice could understand was the word *non*, repeated several times and loudly.

Jack came out of the château, followed by Harry. Neither seemed to be in a particularly good mood. Alice suddenly had a sense of foreboding. This wasn't promising to be a jolly adventure.

Jack made a feeble attempt at a smile.

'Everyone ready to go?'

They all got into the car – Alice, Harry and Callum in the back, while Nathalie took her place by Jack in the front. Claudine squeezed in next to her.

'I think you'll like Montmartre,' Jack said. 'It's not like any other neighbourhood in Paris.' He turned to Nathalie. 'Don't you think so?'

'I go shopping,' Nathalie said. 'Not in Montmartre.'

Jack shifted into reverse so violently the car lurched.

'Whatever,' he murmured.

They left the château grounds in silence.

Chapter Twelve

From the window, Lara watched Jack's car pull away. She'd caught a glimpse of Harry's expression as he walked out and she knew he wasn't happy about this. Well, that was just too bad.

'You do not go to Montmartre with the others?'

Christophe had come up behind her, and she turned to him. 'No. I thought I should stay here and greet some relatives who are coming today.'

'But you will see them tonight,' Christophe said. 'We will all have dinner together here at the château. So there is no need to stay here all day.'

'True,' she admitted.

'Good. Then we spend the day together.'

It was exactly what she'd hoped he would say. 'OK! What will we do?'

He smiled. 'We will go to Paris, and we will have a

typically Parisian day. I will make some lunch reservations and we shall have a nice walk.'

'Sounds perfect,' she said.

'We can leave as soon as you are ready.'

'Ready for what?' Then she noticed his eyes sweep over her jeans and T-shirt. 'Oh – don't I look OK?'

'You look lovely,' he quickly assured her. 'But I want to take you to a very nice place for lunch, so perhaps something a bit more elegant would be appropriate. That dress you wore last night? It was so charming.'

Lara happily agreed. This was like a dream, to be with a man who was so attentive, who actually noticed what she wore. And when she returned, wearing the black dress, the look in Christophe's eyes erased any remnant of guilt she'd been feeling about Harry.

A lift carried Alice and the others from the underground car park to street level. She was relieved to be out of the car – there hadn't been much conversation. Even Harry had been unusually quiet. She tried to pretend it was because they were all tired after last night's late dinner, but she knew it was more than that. Nobody seemed to be in great spirits. Callum seemed lost in his own thoughts. And Jack was clearly tense.

And she knew she couldn't chalk the atmosphere up

to typical pre-wedding jitters. There was nothing typical about this wedding.

'Are you sure you don't want to come with us?' Jack asked Nathalie as they emerged from the lift.

'I am sure,' Nathalie told him. 'I am to be married tomorrow! There is much I must buy.'

Jack looked a little alarmed. 'Remember, you don't need to buy a tiara. *Maman* is going to lend one to you.'

'*Oui*, I remember. But there are other things . . .' She drew Jack aside and spoke softly in French. Jack seemed to clench his teeth for a moment but he didn't say anything. He reached into his pocket and took out his wallet. He handed Nathalie some notes, and then, after she whispered to him again, he gave her a credit card. Suddenly, Nathalie looked a lot more cheerful.

'*Merci, mon amour!*' She wriggled her fingers in a little goodbye salute, linked arms with Claudine and they hurried away. Jack stared after her for a moment, and then turned back to the others.

'We'll take the Métro to Montmartre,' he told them.

The Métro was crowded and noisy, so they couldn't talk, but during the fifteen minutes underground, something happened to Jack. By the time they left the train, his mood had improved remarkably.

'I want you to notice this station,' he told them. 'Abbesses is one of the deepest in Paris. We could take the lift, but then you'll miss something special. Are you up for two hundred steps?'

The climb was well worth the effort. The walls were covered with colourful murals. They passed paintings of Paris sights, windmills, flowers, visions of winged horses – they oohed and ahhed their way up the stairs.

'Montmartre has always been a magnet for artists and bohemian types,' Jack explained as they came out of the station. 'It's like a distinct little village. It's full of tourists now but it hasn't lost its charm. There's something just around the corner I want to show you.' They found themselves in a pretty garden square, dominated by a wall of deep-blue glazed tiles with engraved words.

'It's called the wall of love,' Jack told them. 'They say "I love you" in over three hundred languages. Nice, huh?'

'How romantic,' Alice said, and tried to ignore the stab of sadness that pierced her heart. She remembered who was standing by her side. Quickly, she took Callum's hand and squeezed it. He looked at her . . . but he didn't squeeze back. She glanced at him questioningly but he'd turned his attention to the gardens.

165

Harry took out his phone and started tapping the screen.

'Lara?' Alice asked, and smiled when he nodded. Obviously, the romantic wall had touched him too.

But then he grimaced. 'Straight to voicemail,' he muttered. He stuck the phone back in his pocket without leaving a message.

As they wandered the little twisting streets, Jack talked about the artists who'd lived and painted in Montmartre – Picasso, Van Gogh, Monet – and pointed out buildings that had once been their studios. Alice had forgotten what a big art fan he'd been. Listening to him now, she was more struck by his animated mood than the actual information. She hadn't heard him talk so much, or with so much enthusiasm, since they arrived. This was the Jack she knew – lively and exuberant. He seemed lighter, freer . . . and the strangest image popped into her head. A prisoner who'd just been released from his shackles. It was a bizarre way to think of someone who was about to be married.

She was pleased to see him in a better mood, but he wasn't acting much like someone who was getting married in twenty-four hours. He wasn't excited, or nervous, or anything like that. Why would he be? If he wasn't in love, if he was being forced into a marriage he didn't want . . . but then, she would have expected him to act more depressed. Maybe he was just trying to forget for a while.

She wished she could have some time alone with him, to find out what was going on in his heart, and his mind. The memory of the word '*maman*' on Nathalie's mobile screen came back to her. What did Jack really know about Nathalie? And what had brought them together in the first place? That was the big question. And one she didn't want to contemplate now.

They took a tram called a funicular up the hill to Sacré-Coeur, the big white-domed church at the top of Montmartre. From the top of the stairs they had a panoramic view of Paris.

'We're even higher here than we were at the top of the Eiffel Tower,' Jack told them.

'It's quite a city,' Callum acknowledged. 'Are you going to miss it if you move back to England?'

'*When* I move back,' Jack said with a grin. 'Being around you guys for the past couple of days has made me realize how very much I miss home.'

'You don't think of Paris as home?' Callum asked.

'I love Paris,' Jack said. 'But it's never really been home. I'm half French, but I always felt more English. The culture, the history, the traditions . . . I even prefer the food.'

That comment caught Harry's attention. 'Good for you,' he interjected. 'There's nothing wrong with English food.'

'Every Christmas that I spend in France, I wake up with a craving for Yorkshire pudding,' Jack admitted. 'I think, in the back of my mind, I knew I would settle down back in England. Yeah, I'm definitely English.'

'But you're marrying a French girl,' Callum said.

Jack's grin wavered. 'Yes, I am.'

'Can Nathalie make a Yorkshire pudding?' Harry asked.

The smile was gone now. Jack stared out at the view with eyes that didn't seem to be seeing anything. 'Nathalie can't cook,' he said. Then, as if realizing that he sounded like he was criticizing her, he quickly added, 'But of course, she never had parents to teach her.'

Again, Alice envisioned the word on the mobile screen. But all she said was, 'You always liked cooking.'

'True,' Jack said. 'Remember when we got those amazing oranges and spent a whole day making marmalade?'

Alice nodded. 'And we ended up giving it all away because neither of us liked marmalade.'

'I can see you and Nathalie now,' Harry said. 'Whipping up homemade jam to sell at the village fête.'

168

'Maybe,' Jack murmured without much conviction. Then he shook his head, as if he was shaking off negative thoughts. 'Hey, this conversation is making me hungry. Who wants lunch?'

'I hope you are hungry,' Christophe said. 'We go to lunch now.'

They were passing cafés along the banks of the Seine and Lara wondered if they'd be stopping at one of them. There were a lot of people sitting on the terraces in the sunshine, and she caught glimpses of meals that looked delicious.

At the same time, she kept looking over her shoulder.

'Is something wrong?' Christophe asked.

'I'm just afraid we'll run into the others,' Lara said.

'Do not worry,' Christophe told her. 'We are not near Montmartre.' He cocked his head and looked at her with interest. 'Would your boyfriend be very jealous if he knew we were together?'

Lara shook her head. 'Harry isn't the jealous type. He wouldn't care.'

'I find that hard to believe,' Christophe said. 'If you were my girlfriend, I would be furious if any other man approached you. I think you are a woman worth fighting for.'

She knew he was joking, but she appreciated his extravagant gallantry. 'Harry isn't much of a fighter.'

'Not even for you?'

'I don't know,' she admitted honestly.

'It is a serious relationship?' he asked.

How could she answer that? She hadn't been out with anyone else since meeting Harry. She hadn't even looked at another man. Well, that wasn't exactly true. She could admire a man who was particularly good-looking, or interesting, just like she admired Christophe. But she'd never felt really attracted to anyone else since she'd met Harry.

Until now . . .

'We're not engaged, or anything like that,' she finally said. 'I mean, we haven't talked about the future.'

'I am very happy to hear that.' Christophe's light tone had suddenly become less light. Startled, she looked at him. He was gazing at her with an intensity that made her nervous.

'Come, we cross to the Left Bank now,' he said. They turned on to a bridge and he indicated a building on the other side.

'This is where we are having lunch. La Tour d'Argent – one of the oldest and grandest restaurants in Paris.'

She took in the imposing champagne-coloured

building. 'Wow, that looks smart. I hope I'm dressed OK.'

'You're lovely,' Christophe assured her. 'You look . . .' He gazed upwards, as if he was searching for the perfect word. 'You look French.'

Lara got the impression this was the ultimate compliment.

Below them, on the river, one of those big sightseeing boats floated by. She knew it was packed with tourists like her, gaping out at the romance and beauty of Paris. Just like she'd done only the day before yesterday. But now, here she was, with a real Frenchman, going to a real French restaurant and actually looking like a Frenchwoman herself. She felt as if a magic wand had been raised and had turned her into another person.

Inside the building, a lift took them to the sixth floor. There they were greeted by a man in a black suit who tipped his head in a slight bow and spoke to them warmly. He then led them into the most elegant restaurant Lara had ever seen in her life. Under an ornately carved domed ceiling with a massive glittering chandelier, diners sat at tables covered in yellow cloths that looked golden under the light coming from the broad windows. Here and there, large antique bowls held enormous bouquets of orange and yellow roses.

Lara was no authority on tableware, but passing the

tables she knew she was seeing real crystal, sterling silver cutlery, bone china plates. At a little table by a window, the waiter pulled out a chair for her.

She was in awe, and it must have shown on her face because Christophe looked amused. 'What do you think?' he asked.

'It's so, so . . .' She searched for the right word. The ultimate compliment came back to her. 'It's so *French*!'

The waiter returned with menus and a huge book that looked as if it belonged to a set of encyclopaedias.

'What's that?' she asked.

'The wine list,' Christophe told her. 'La Tour d'Argent has one of the greatest wine cellars in Paris.' He opened his menu, and she opened hers.

She'd decided on their way to the restaurant that she'd be careful about what she ordered. She knew she could safely assume that he was treating her to this meal but she didn't want to seem greedy so she planned to order something that wasn't terribly expensive. There was a problem though.

'What's wrong?' Christophe asked.

'There are no prices on the menu!'

He chuckled. 'That is the tradition in fine French restaurants, Lara. Only the gentleman's menu includes prices.'

'But what if the woman is paying?'

He gave a little shrug. 'That is unheard of in a place like this.'

She'd wanted to appear sophisticated, knowledgeable, stylish and worldly, and now she felt unrefined and naive. And she was bound to make more stupid mistakes like this. Dimly, she recalled a novel in which a character had faced a finger bowl at a dinner for the first time and had mistaken it for a bowl of soup. It sounded like something she would do. She, who had called Harry a peasant . . .

And what if she dropped something on herself? She had a tendency to do that. Sometimes she could be as bad as Harry.

In despair, she stared down at the menu and tried to make sense of the French words.

'Lara?'

She looked up.

'Shall I order for both of us?'

'Yes, please.' And then she blurted out, 'I've never been to a place like this in my life.'

Had she just blown it by revealing her ignorance like this? Lara watched his expression anxiously. But the smile that crossed his face wasn't at all disdainful.

'Lara, you are so very, very charming. Lara . . . the

name suits you. Is it Russian?'

'I think so. My mother loved the film *Doctor Zhivago* and she named me after a character in it. But there's nothing Russian about my family. I'm just an ordinary English girl.'

'Oh no, not at all,' he said. 'Perhaps, by birth and ancestry. But in your heart, you are European.'

'Of course I'm European! Great Britain is in Europe, you know. Even if we don't use the euro.'

He laughed. 'I should have said "continental". I don't mean to criticize your people. But you don't seem like a fish and chips girl to me.'

She wished he hadn't mentioned fish and chips. A memory popped into her head – a September weekend jaunt to Suffolk. She and Harry had stopped in Aldeburgh, a small seaside town on the East Suffolk coast, picked up some fish and chips, and eaten them walking along the windy beach. They'd both agreed they were the best fish and chips they'd ever had . . .

But maybe she was about to have an even more memorable meal. So she firmly pushed the fish, the chips and Harry from her mind, and tried to understand as Christophe spoke to the waiter.

The first course arrived soon after. On both their plates rested a scoop of something glossy and pale brown, with what looked like jellied condiments on the side of the plate.

'What is it?' Lara asked.

'Taste it first,' Christophe urged.

She dipped her fork into the soft mound and put it in her mouth. It was silky and smooth and it tasted like nothing she'd ever eaten before.

'It's delicious!' she exclaimed. 'Now will you tell me what it is?'

'Foie gras,' Christophe said. 'Goose liver. A great French delicacy.'

It sounded familiar, and then she remembered where she'd heard about it – at St Pancras, when Harry was complaining about French food.

Watching her face, Christophe frowned. 'Now, please don't tell me you're one of those people who are opposed to the creation of foie gras.'

'It's cruel to the animals, isn't it?'

Christophe gave that little shrug again. She was beginning to think this must be the male version of Nathalie's pout.

'Foie gras is part of the cultural heritage of France,' he declared firmly. 'Come now, Lara. Don't disappoint me. If you're French in your heart, you will indulge your senses and enjoy this luxury.'

She certainly didn't want to disappoint him. And she was his guest; she couldn't insult his heritage.

'Oh well,' she sighed. 'It's not like I ever had a pet goose.'

Christophe looked at her curiously. 'I don't understand.'

'I'm just saying, I'd feel worse if this was made of rabbit. Because I once had a pet rabbit.'

He still didn't seem to get it so Lara gave up. She dipped her fork into the foie gras again, added a bit of the condiment and took another bite. And that delicious taste, along with Christophe's smile of approval, pretty much wiped out any concern for what might have been done to the goose.

'How are your crêpes?' Jack asked.

The four of them were strolling along one of the twisting cobbled Montmartre streets while they ate lunch.

'Delicious,' Alice said. 'How about yours, Cal?'

'Yes, very nice.'

'It's good, but there's not much to it,' Harry said. 'I could eat another one.'

'There are crêpe places all over Montmartre,' Jack told him. 'Look, there's another one just at the corner.'

Harry ambled over to the little food stall.

'I'm glad to see his mood isn't affecting his appetite,' Callum remarked.

'What's the matter with him anyway?' Jack asked. 'He seems kind of down.'

'I think he's upset that Lara didn't come with us,' Alice said.

'Oh. Are they having problems?'

'I'm not sure,' she replied. 'Has he said anything to you?' she asked Callum.

Callum shook his head. He smiled, but it wasn't his usual broad grin. 'Boys don't talk to each other like that.'

'True,' Jack said. And Alice couldn't help noticing that both of them wore similar expressions. There was a moment of silence.

'You know, I could go for another crêpe myself,' said Jack. 'Anyone else want one?'

Neither Callum nor Alice took him up on the offer, and remained standing there as Jack went to join Harry. Callum was still wearing that wistful expression and Alice could see that *he* wasn't in the best mood either.

'Are you worried about Harry?'

'Not really,' he said. 'I saw Lara hanging out a lot with that French guy last night, but I don't think it means anything. They'll be OK.'

'I think so too,' Alice said.

'I'm not so sure about the bride and groom though.'

Alice gazed after Jack's figure. 'I know what you mean. They don't really seem suited, do they?'

'No.' After a pause, he said, 'And what about us?'

Startled, Alice turned to face him directly. 'Us?'

'You and me. Are we suited, Alice?'

She struggled for words. 'Well . . . we get along, don't we? Of course, it's only been a couple of months . . .' She was relieved to see Jack beckoning to them. 'I think our presence is required. Come on.'

The corner where Jack and Harry had bought their crêpes led on to a large, open square, surrounded by cafés and shops, mostly selling souvenirs. Alice was struck by the easels set up around the periphery, and the painters who worked on canvases.

'Is there an art class going on?' she asked Jack.

'No, this is the Place du Tertre. It's always been a hangout for artists. They paint here and sell their works.'

They wandered around the square, checking out the artists' creative efforts. Some were really good, others just so-so, but it was fun to look at everything. About every third person invited them to sit for portraits.

'I'd kill for a coffee right now,' Jack announced. He led

them to one of the cafés, where they could sit on the terrace and watch the artists. 'So, what do you think of Montmartre?'

'I like it,' Alice said. 'Nathalie was right, it's full of tourists, but it's still fun to see. It was cool seeing the real Moulin Rouge.' She turned to Callum. 'Did you see the film?'

'No.'

'I can't even remember when it came out, it was so long ago,' Alice said. 'We were all just kids.' A memory made her laugh. 'Jack, remember?'

Jack made a dramatic gesture, placing his hand on his heart and gazing upwards. '"The greatest thing you'll ever learn, is just to love and be loved in return."'

Laughing, Alice explained to Callum and Harry. 'My mum took us to see it because she'd heard it was a musical. But it turned out to be pretty sexy. Jack kept making gagging sounds all through it.'

'And you kept shushing me,' Jack said. 'I couldn't believe you were so into it. The whole thing was unbelievably corny.'

'It was romantic!' Alice exclaimed. 'We should watch it again some time, on DVD. Maybe you're mature enough to appreciate it now.'

'I sincerely doubt it,' Jack said.

'You doubt what? The quality of the movie or your own maturity?'

'Look who's talking about maturity! I bet you're still sleeping with that teddy bear I won for you.'

Harry suddenly stood up. 'I need to make a phone call.' He took out his mobile and walked away.

'Oops,' Alice said. 'We made him think about Lara. They tease each other like that all the time, right, Cal?'

'Yes,' Callum said in a flat voice. 'They're always doing that.'

Just then, a man wearing a beret and a paint-splashed jacket approached them. In his hand was a sheet of paper.

'*Excusez-moi, mademoiselle, messieurs,*' he said. Then he switched to strongly accented English. 'I see you, and I think, they are so much in love! I feel it, here.' He touched his heart. 'You inspire me, so I draw picture for you. I try to capture the feelings you have.'

Callum reached into his pocket and pulled out his wallet but the artist shook his head violently. '*Non, non!* I cannot take money for this. It comes from the soul. I give it freely to the young lovers.' Gently, he laid the paper on their table, and then he scurried away.

Alice drew in her breath sharply. The man was clearly talented. He'd created a very good likeness of her.

180

And of Jack.

Her gasp was the only sound at the table. Then the silence was broken by Jack's mobile. He snatched up his phone quickly, as if desperate for something to break the tension.

'*Allo?*'

Alice saw his forehead crease and his eyebrows come together in a sign of concern.

'*Qu'est que c'est? Comment? D'accord.*' He put the phone in his pocket and stood up.

'That was Nathalie. She's run into some kind of problem and she needs me to go and get her.'

'Is she OK?' Alice asked.

'I don't know! She's not hurt, but she said it's an emergency. Look, you stay here and I'll call you when I find out what's going on.'

He took off, and Alice was left alone with Callum.

And the picture.

She picked it up and tried to think of something to say.

'Stupid artist,' she murmured.

Callum was silent for a moment. Then he said, 'Maybe not that stupid.'

And Alice burst into tears.

* * *

'Do you know Rodin?' Christophe asked as they entered the garden of the museum dedicated to him.

'Not personally,' Lara said. 'He's more like a friend of a friend.'

Christophe looked at her blankly.

'But you could not know him personally, Lara. He died almost a hundred years ago.'

'I was joking!'

He still looked puzzled. She crossed 'sense of humour' off his list of many attributes. He was still gorgeous, charming, smart and incredibly polite, so the absence of one quality didn't make much of a dent.

'But you have heard of Rodin?' he asked.

'Of course. I took Introduction to Art History last term. He was a sculptor.'

'He was the first great modern sculptor,' Christophe corrected her. 'And the greatest French sculptor of his time. Or any time, in my opinion.'

Since Lara couldn't name any other sculptors at the moment, she accepted that. 'Oh, I recognize this!' she cried in delight as they paused before the figure of a naked seated man, his elbow on his knee and his head resting on his hand.

'Yes, this is one of the most well-known works. *The Thinker*.'

Lara couldn't help herself – a memory came to mind and she began to giggle.

'What's funny?' Christophe asked.

'I was just remembering my lecture, back at uni. The lecturer was showing slides, and when this one came on the screen he didn't tell us the name straight away. He asked if any of us knew what it was called. When no one said anything, he asked us what we thought the man was doing. And some bloke called out, "He's on the toilet".'

Christophe raised an eyebrow, and that stopped the giggles. Oh great, she thought in despair. Now he thinks I'm vulgar, like Harry. How could she make up for it?

She walked over to face another large work, and gazed at it with an expression that she hoped reflected intelligent contemplation.

'This is lovely,' she said.

Christophe joined her in front of the sculpture of a naked man and woman locked in an embrace.

'*The Kiss*,' Christophe said reverently. 'Lovers, joined for eternity. If one had no knowledge of Rodin at all, it would be impossible to mistake his nationality.'

'What do you mean?'

He smiled kindly. 'Only a Frenchman would understand love so well that he could create a work like this.'

Lara grinned. 'Oh, come on, Christophe. The French don't have a monopoly on love.'

'No. But we have perfected the art.'

She searched his eyes for a hint that he was having her on. But he seemed totally serious.

'What about French women?' she asked him. 'Do you think they understand love better than other women?'

'Of course,' he said. He smiled. 'But do not worry, Lara. As I told you earlier, I believe you are French in your heart.'

She was thinking about someone else. 'What about a French woman with an English man?' she asked. 'Like Jack and Nathalie?'

'Jack is half French,' he reminded her.

'Does that mean they'll be joined for half an eternity?' she joked.

He shook his head. 'I predict they are together for a year.'

'Really? That's all?'

'Well, at least nine months,' he said with an unmistakable smirk.

'Nine months,' Lara repeated. The implication hit her. 'Oh, you know that she's pregnant, huh?'

'Jack told me. I suppose I should not have said this. I

presume she would prefer that people believe they are marrying for love.'

'You don't think Jack's in love with her? I suppose you'd know, being his best man.'

He shrugged.

Lara pressed him. 'But he must have feelings for her. If she's having a baby, then they must have been having some kind of relationship.'

'A man can make a big mistake,' Christophe said.

Lara was intrigued. 'You mean it was a one-night stand, something like that?'

Christophe looked as if he was dying to say more, but he shook his head. 'I cannot speak of this.'

'Why not?' Lara pressed. 'I'm Jack's cousin and I care about him! You're his friend, you must care too. From the minute I met Nathalie, I didn't think she was Jack's type.'

'She is nobody's type,' Christophe blurted out. 'Who could love a woman like that?'

'Do you know her very well?' Lara asked.

'We are from the same village in the south,' he told her.

She was surprised. 'Really? Were you friends?'

'Not at all,' he said quickly. 'Now, let us go inside the museum and look at the drawings.'

And as they moved in that direction, he added, 'I am bored speaking of Jack and Nathalie. I would rather speak of us.'

Chapter Thirteen

Fortunately, the hordes of people in the Montmartre square were too busy watching the artists work and taking photographs to notice a weeping girl at a café table. With her face covered by her hands, Alice couldn't see Callum's reaction to her sudden breakdown. But she felt his gentle touch on her shoulder. He didn't say anything, but the touch spoke words.

When she'd recovered enough to take her hands away, she searched through her handbag for a tissue. She wiped her eyes, blew her nose and summoned up the strength to face Callum.

'I'm sorry,' she whispered.

'So am I,' he replied.

'I don't know what brought that on,' she said. 'Maybe I'm just exhausted or something . . .'

'Alice, stop it. Don't invent excuses.'

His face was a blur through her tear-stained eyes, but she could still make out his kind, sad expression.

'I think I've known from the moment we arrived,' he continued. 'You still have feelings for Jack. I could see it, in the way you looked at him, the way you spoke.'

She wanted to protest, to deny it, but she knew her words wouldn't ring true. 'I thought it was over . . .' she murmured.

'Some feelings never die,' Callum said. 'Like love. You still love him, Alice. I saw it, long before that artist did. I just didn't want to admit it to myself.'

'But it's crazy,' she said weakly. 'And it's wrong, it's so wrong. Cal, you're the best thing that's ever happened to me. I can't let these stupid feelings come between us.'

'Alice, I don't blame you, and I can't be angry. We can't choose who we fall in love with. And love isn't always logical.'

She definitely couldn't argue with that. Here she was with this great guy, who was smart and kind and understanding. The kind of guy any normal girl would be thrilled to have as a boyfriend. And she couldn't think about anyone except a childhood sweetheart who belonged to someone else.

'I was thinking I was in love with you,' Callum went on. 'But I know the feeling isn't mutual.'

'Oh, Cal, I do care about you, so much!'

'I believe you. But you don't love me. Do you, Alice?'

She wanted to say something like, 'Not yet, give it time.' But she knew he was right.

'I'll tell you something else too,' Callum said. 'Jack's still in love with you.'

She shook her head violently. 'He's getting married tomorrow!'

Callum offered her a small smile. 'He doesn't love her. You've been around them for a couple of days. You must be able to see that.'

'But he's marrying her,' she said. 'So it doesn't matter. I can't be in love with a married man.'

'He's not married yet,' Callum said.

She looked at him in bewilderment. 'What are you saying?'

'Maybe he doesn't know how you feel. It's not too late, you know. Talk to him.'

'She's having his baby, Cal! Jack's not going to leave her!'

'Not now,' Callum said. 'But maybe, in the future . . .' His voice trailed off.

She gazed at him in wonderment. There was hurt and pain all over his face, and yet here he was, advising her to tell another man she loved him. She gripped his hand as shame and guilt washed over her.

'Oh, Cal. I didn't mean for this to happen. I can't believe I'm doing this to you.'

'It's OK,' he said lightly. 'I'll survive.'

'I wasn't using you, you know. I liked you so much, and I thought this would turn into love. But . . . maybe it just wasn't meant to be.'

'I understand,' he said.

'We can still be friends?' she asked.

'Of course,' he replied. He got up and nodded in the direction of a shop across the square. 'I think I'll go and get a couple of souvenirs.'

Like he'll really want to remember this weekend, Alice thought as she watched him walk away. Any more than she would.

Harry came out of the café. She'd almost forgotten about him. He plonked himself down on a seat across from Alice.

'Where are the others?'

'Nathalie called and said she had some kind of emergency, so Jack went to get her. Cal's buying souvenirs.'

'Want a coffee?' Harry asked.

Alice nodded, and he waved to a waiter. After placing the order, he slumped back in his seat. He didn't comment on Alice's red eyes. Clearly, he was too caught up in his own mood to notice hers.

'I can't reach Lara. I've left her two messages and she hasn't called back.'

'She must be busy,' Alice offered lamely. At least he was providing a distraction from her own feelings.

He drummed his fingers on the table. 'Something's wrong.'

As if on cue, Alice's mobile made a beeping sound. She took it out of her bag.

'I've got a text message from her!' She hit a button and read the message silently.

`I just ate foie gras! Don't tell Harry! And I've got some news!`

Alice stared at the message. What did that last line mean? Had something happened between Lara and Christophe?

'What did she say?' Harry asked anxiously.

Quickly, Alice deleted the message. 'She just wants to know how we're doing, and when we're coming back to the château.'

Harry took out his own mobile and looked at the screen. 'She didn't text *me*.'

'Well, at least you know she's OK.'

'Yeah,' Harry said glumly. 'I know she's alive. I guess

that's some comfort.' His normally bright eyes seemed dull as they focused pleadingly on Alice. 'What's wrong with her? She's been acting weird.'

'I'm not sure what you mean,' Alice said carefully.

'Come on, Alice. Something's up. Do you think she's with *him*?'

She stalled for time. 'Who?'

'Christophe!' He practically spat out the word. 'I've seen them talking. And I've seen the way she looks at him.'

She tried to make light of it. 'Hey, any girl would enjoy looking at Christophe, Harry.'

'That's not what I mean and you know it,' he muttered.

This was getting uncomfortable, and she didn't know what to say. She didn't want to lie but she wouldn't betray her best friend.

'Look, I get it,' Harry said. 'He's everything I'm not. He's got the looks, and he's got the charm . . .' His eyes darkened. 'I'll bet he's got the moves too.' He picked up his coffee, took a sip and made a face. 'It's cold.'

'Lara just enjoys meeting people,' Alice said.

'Yeah, I know . . . but she could be falling for him.' He looked at her in desperation. 'I can't lose her, Alice. She means everything to me.'

'Have you ever told her that?' Alice asked.

'Are you crazy? She'd laugh!'

There was a time when she would have agreed with him. Lara was never into sentimental talk. But now . . .

'I'm not so sure about that.' She leaned forward. 'Harry, Lara loves you. And you love her. It wouldn't hurt if you actually talked about the way you feel. And it might help.'

He still looked doubtful. 'You and Cal talk about stuff like that?'

She hesitated. Maybe she should wait for Callum to tell his friend what had just happened between them. 'We're honest about our feelings,' she said finally.

Harry fell silent. 'You know, from the moment I met her, I knew she was the one. She knew it too, I'm sure of that. We never had to say anything. It was like . . . we belonged together. I – I can't imagine a life without her.'

She'd never heard Harry talk like this before. And she was absolutely, positively sure that Lara hadn't either.

'Tell her, Harry.'

'I don't know if I can,' he said. 'Anyway, it might be too late.'

And I've got some news.

He might be right, Alice thought.

Callum returned, and held up a little bag. 'Eiffel Tower keyrings,' he announced. 'Enough to satisfy Secret Santa obligations at the bank for the next ten years. Hey, that coffee looks good.' He waved to a waiter. '*Un café, s'il vous plaît.*'

He sounds just a tad too happy, Alice thought. He was putting on an act.

Callum sat down. 'Hey, my man, you're looking grim. What's up?'

Alice wondered if she should find an excuse to leave the table for a while, so he and Harry could share their problems. Callum had said guys didn't talk about their personal feelings, but there had to be exceptions to that rule.

But there wasn't time anyway. Jack and Nathalie were coming towards them. And *they* didn't look very happy either. Jack's brow was creased and he was clearly in a state of annoyance. Nathalie was pouting.

'Is everything all right?' Alice asked in alarm.

'Do you want to tell them about your emergency, Nathalie?' Jack asked through gritted teeth.

Nathalie stopped pouting and took on a look of aggrieved innocence as she addressed the others.

'A bride, she must have a trousseau, yes? New things to wear? I see a beautiful *sac à main* . . .'

'A handbag,' Jack interjected.

'And to pay, I give *la carte de crédit*.'

Jack broke in again. 'My credit card.'

'And the woman who sells, she says to me, it is not good!'

Jack explained. 'My line of credit doesn't extend to two thousand euros.'

Alice gasped. 'Two thousand euros for a handbag?'

Nathalie was quick to justify the expense. 'It is a handbag of Christian Dior!'

Harry too was shocked. 'That was your big emergency?' he asked.

Nathalie resumed her pout and said nothing.

'Where's Claudine?' Alice asked.

'She's meeting us at the car. Are you guys ready to leave?' Jack asked.

'Absolutely,' Callum said.

'Totally,' Harry echoed.

Alice had no objection either. She suspected none of them could continue appreciating the charm of Montmartre.

Chapter Fourteen

A sense of gloom permeated the car, and no one said much as Jack drove them back to the château. Jack complained about the traffic, Callum made a half-hearted comment about the Arc de Triomphe, Harry offered a feeble joke about French driving habits, but that was about it. Claudine clamped on her earphones and listened to music. Nathalie stared out of the window, looking bored.

Once again in the back seat between Harry and Callum, Alice could feel the weight of all the low spirits. Or maybe she was just contemplating her own – they were heavy enough to wear her down.

Her head was spinning with question marks. Thank goodness they were nearing the château. If Lara had already returned, Alice could throw herself into convincing her that Harry was her one true love, and work on putting things right between them. And hopefully, stop thinking about herself and a situation she had no control over at all.

Lara *was* back, and she must have been watching for them from a window; Jack hadn't even parked the car before she came running out of the château. As everyone got out, Lara didn't bother to greet them. She clutched Alice's arm.

'We have to talk!'

'Hi,' Harry said, but Lara didn't even hear him. Alice caught a glimpse of his stricken face before Lara dragged her away.

They went around to the back of the château.

'I've got something to tell you,' Lara began.

'I've got something to tell you too,' Alice said, thinking about everything that had happened at the café.

'Me first,' Lara insisted. 'Christophe told me something.'

'Oh no,' Alice groaned. 'Lara . . . did he say he's in love with you?'

'What? No, nothing like that. It's about Jack and Nathalie.'

'What?'

'He says Jack isn't in love with her, and there was never really any kind of relationship between them. He wouldn't tell me a lot but I got the impression that it was pretty much a one-night stand. I believe him too. I mean, he's Jack's best man, he has to know him pretty well.'

Alice sighed. 'This is even sadder than I thought.'

'But aren't you glad to know he never loved her?'

'Not really,' Alice said. 'I'm thinking about Jack. Trapped in a loveless marriage. How awful for him. Well, I've got some news too. Cal and I broke up.'

'Oh, no!' Lara wailed.

Alice told her about the artist in Montmartre, and her reaction to his drawing. 'Cal could see I still have feelings for Jack.'

'Maybe it's for the best,' Lara ventured.

'Who knows,' said Alice. 'We might have gone on, and I would have convinced myself that I loved him. We could have ended up in a loveless marriage too.' She smiled slightly. 'Some romantic weekend, huh?'

She looked up as she heard someone approach. An unsmiling Nathalie came towards them.

'Lara, Jack tells me, you must come. Your people arrive.'

'My people? Oh, you mean Jack's father and the others.' She turned to Alice. 'I should go. I'll see you back in the room.'

Alice was looking at a certain area of Nathalie's body. Even in the figure-hugging dress, she couldn't see any sign of her condition. But it was early days.

She went back into the château and up the stairs. Callum was in their room. His small suitcase was on one of the lower bunk beds, and it was open. She stood in the doorway and watched as he gathered up some clothes and put them in it.

'What are you doing?' she asked.

'What does it look like?' he asked back with a light tone that took the edge off any sarcasm.

She sat down on the opposite bed. 'You're leaving.'

He nodded as he carefully folded a shirt. 'I've called a taxi to take me back to Paris. It might even be here already.'

'But why? There's no need for you to go. We're still friends, we can still have a good time . . .' Her voice trailed off as he turned away from the suitcase and actually looked at her.

'I know,' she said. 'It's not exactly a fun weekend. Cal . . . do you hate me?'

'No, I don't hate you, Alice. And yeah, sure, maybe we can still be friends, but right now . . . I'd rather be alone.'

She could feel her eyes beginning to well up again. She wasn't sure who she would be crying for – Callum, Jack or herself. All of them, probably.

Callum closed the suitcase. 'I know you feel bad, Alice,

and I'm not trying to make you feel worse. Like I told you before, I'll survive. But I'm not really in the mood to hang around here now. Surely you can understand that.'

She could. She didn't want to hang around here either any more. She couldn't leave – but Callum had only come because of her. Now, there was nothing to keep him here.

'I understand,' she said.

He closed the suitcase. 'Have a nice weekend.'

She nodded. 'Cal . . . we can still get together sometimes, can't we?'

'Yes,' he said. 'Maybe not right away though.'

She understood that too. He came over, bent down and kissed her forehead. 'I hope it works out for you.'

It can't, it's not even a possibility, she thought. But aloud, she said, 'For you too.'

And then he was gone. She remained seated on the bed and tried to make some sense of everything that had happened.

A few moments later, the door opened and Lara came in.

'I just saw Cal getting into a taxi with a suitcase.'

'Yeah. He didn't want to stick around. I can't say I blame him.' She fell back on the bed. 'I sort of wish I could leave myself. I've never been to a wedding where everyone's miserable. Jack, Cal, me, Harry—'

'Harry's miserable?' Lara asked sharply.

'He's afraid something's going on between you and Christophe. He's really worried, Lara. He told me when we were in Montmartre.'

There was a moment of silence, and then Lara said, 'Good.'

Alice stared at her. '*Good?* You're glad he's miserable?'

'I'm glad he's actually paying attention,' Lara said.

'Lara . . . *is* there something going on between you and Christophe?'

Lara seemed to be choosing her words carefully. 'If you're asking, have we kissed or anything, then no. But I wouldn't mind if Harry thinks we did.'

'Lara, that's cruel. You don't mean that. You don't want Harry to suffer.'

'I'm just sick of being taken for granted!' Lara burst out. 'Being with someone like Christophe, it's so – so *different*.'

'You had a nice day with him?'

'Wonderful. He took me to this incredibly posh restaurant on the Left Bank. He's really classy, Alice. I mean, he knows about wine, and art, and music. But he's not a snob! He didn't mock me when I told her I'd never been to a real ballet. And he invited me to come back to Paris in the autumn, when the opera season starts, so he can take me to one.'

Alice looked at her through narrowed eyes. 'Since when are you interested in opera? You don't even like classical music.'

'Well, maybe I could learn to like it,' Lara retorted. 'He's special, Alice! We walked through the Luxembourg Gardens and I swear I felt like I was in a French movie. It was like a fantasy.'

'Exactly,' Alice said. 'A fantasy. Not real life.'

'For some people it's real life,' Lara remarked defensively. 'Christophe, he's so attentive. Harry barely looks at me, and half the time I don't think he even hears what I'm saying. Christophe pays me compliments, he looks at me like I'm the only girl in the world . . .'

'Harry thinks you're the only girl in the world, Lara. He told me he couldn't live without you.'

'Well, he certainly doesn't show it.' She got up and moved restlessly around the room.

'You don't think you would actually leave Harry for Christophe, do you?' Alice asked anxiously. 'I mean, he's charming and all that, but I can't really see you two together for the long haul.'

'I'm not thinking that far ahead. I'm just having some fun. And don't worry,' she added. 'I'm not going to do anything I'll regret. I certainly don't want to end up like Nathalie and Jack.'

'I should hope not,' Alice said with a shudder.

'I still can't believe Jack's going to be a father,' Lara remarked.

'I bet he'll be a good one,' Alice said wistfully. 'He never got much attention from his father, so he'll go overboard trying to compensate with his own child.'

'Which is a good thing,' Lara said. 'Because I can't see Nathalie as a loving mother.'

'Maybe she'll change,' Alice said, without much hope. 'She might enjoy being a mum.'

'Maybe,' Lara echoed. 'Does Chanel make baby clothes?'

They shared a smile. Then Lara looked at her watch. 'We should start getting ready for the evening. Jack says a few of his friends are joining us for dinner. Maybe there'll be a nice single Frenchman for you.'

'No thanks,' Alice replied tartly. 'I think I'm going to swear off men for a while. They're making me miserable.'

'Did Harry really say he couldn't live without me?' Lara asked suddenly.

'Pretty much.'

'Huh.'

'*Huh?* What does *that* mean?' Alice asked.

'I'm not sure,' Lara replied. 'Just . . . huh.'

Chapter Fifteen

They'd just reached the bottom of the stairs when they heard the shriek. It was coming from the so-called bridal suite, Jack and Nathalie's room. Then they heard Nathalie yelling, practically screaming, in French.

Alice gasped. 'What was that?'

Lara couldn't make out the words, but she didn't need fluent French to recognize the sound of anger. A wonderful possibility occurred to her. 'Maybe they're breaking up!'

But the next voice they heard was Claudine's. She too sounded extremely upset. Alice and Lara moved towards the door. It was slightly ajar, and Lara knocked on it. Her rapping made the door open wider and they could see the two French girls. Claudine was wearing bright-purple taffeta and Nathalie was struggling with the zip.

'What's going on?' Lara asked.

Nathalie was pale with fury. 'Stupid Claudine! Her dress for the wedding, it is too tight!'

'It fit when I tried it last week,' Claudine wailed.

'But then you eat like pig, you get too fat!' Nathalie yelled. 'Now you cannot be maid of honour!'

Claudine burst into tears.

'Wait, maybe there's something else she can wear,' Alice suggested. 'I've got a nice dress she could borrow.'

'Not nice enough for wedding,' Nathalie declared.

'How do you know it's not nice enough?' Lara demanded.

Nathalie turned to her and Lara took a step backwards. She didn't particularly want to become Nathalie's next target. Then Nathalie turned to Alice.

'I think dress will fit you,' she announced. 'You will be maid of honour.'

A torrent of angry French came out of Claudine's mouth. She started pulling at the dress. An ominous sound resulted, and Nathalie screamed.

The dress fell off Claudine, and she stepped out of it. She uttered one French word at Nathalie – Lara assumed it was something pretty vile – grabbed the clothes she'd had on earlier which were piled on a bed, and stormed out of the room in just her underwear.

Nathalie stared at the crumpled taffeta on the floor. 'My wedding,' she moaned. 'It is ruined.'

Alice hurried forward. 'Maybe not.' She picked up the dress and began examining it. Lara meanwhile was trying to drum up some sympathy for the distressed bride but it wasn't easy.

'This really isn't too bad,' Alice said. 'It ripped at the seam. In fact, this might be for the best. It's a wide seam; it could be re-stitched so that it wouldn't be so tight on Claudine.'

'I do not understand,' Nathalie said.

'I think I can fix it!' Alice said. 'Do you have a needle and thread?'

Lara wasn't surprised that Nathalie was not in possession of those items. What did surprise her was Alice offering to help the bride-to-be of the man she loved. Sometimes Alice could be a little too nice. And she would have told her so if Nathalie hadn't been there.

'I've got a little sewing kit upstairs; I'll get it. Lara, go and find Claudine. Tell her it's going to be OK.'

Personally, Lara didn't care if this whole terrible wedding went right down the drain. Hadn't there been enough drama already? But she wasn't about to strike up a debate – if nothing else, they could demonstrate to nasty Nathalie how real friends behaved.

Nathalie, who seemed to have calmed down a bit, directed her to Claudine's room. There, Nathalie found the dismissed maid of honour fully dressed and packing a suitcase.

'I leave now,' Claudine informed her unnecessarily.

'Yeah, I see that. But Alice thinks she can fix the dress so it will fit you.'

'I don't care,' Claudine snapped. 'I will not be maid of honour. I hate Nathalie.'

'Oh, come on, you don't mean that.' Lara sat on the bed. 'You two are best friends, right? Like me and Alice. We bicker, we get into little tiffs. I've lost my temper and said things I didn't really mean; so has she.'

'She tells a lie about me,' Claudine declared. 'I am not fat. I think she shrinks the dress.'

'Why would she lie about you?'

'Because she lies all the time!'

Now, this was interesting. 'What does she lie about?'

'Everything! She tells Jack she is student at university. She is not student! She just works in the student cafeteria. And you know why she takes that job? So she can meet a rich student like Jack. And she says she is orphan. Ha! She is not orphan. She has mother and father.'

'Then . . . why aren't they here?'

'Because she is ashamed. The mother, the father, they are not of the high class.'

'But Jack wouldn't care about something like that!'

'Some boys, they will not want to marry a girl from a family like that. She tells this lie to all the boys.'

Lara groaned. Her opinion of Nathalie, as low as it already was, had sunk to new depths. And not because of her lowly origins. How could a girl lie like that to the man she was about to marry?

'That's really stupid,' she finally said.

There was a knock at the door, and then a voice. 'It's me, Alice.'

Lara opened the door. Alice stood there with her arms full of purple taffeta. 'Claudine, try it on again. I think it will fit now.'

'I am not going to be her maid of honour,' Claudine said. 'I leave now.'

'Now, Claudine, Nathalie's sorry for what she said,' Alice murmured soothingly. 'She's just nervous, all brides get like that. Try the dress on. Please?'

Claudine hesitated. Then she started taking off her clothes.

'See how lovely you look!' Alice exclaimed once the dress was on. She pushed Claudine in front of the mirror. Lara tried to catch her eye but Alice refused to look at her, and Lara knew why. The dress clashed horribly with Claudine's flame-red hair. Alice was almost as good a liar as Nathalie.

'And think of the fun tomorrow,' Alice went on. 'All those people, watching you walk down the aisle. And afterwards, there will be champagne and dancing. You don't want to miss that.'

Lara could see from the French girl's expression that she was weakening. 'Jack, he has invited other boys from the university,' she murmured.

'Yes, lots of boys!' Alice agreed. 'And they will be all over you. The maid of honour is a very important person and everyone looks at her. Think of Pippa Middleton.'

Claudine looked puzzled. 'Who?'

'Never mind. I'm just saying, the maid of honour gets a lot of attention, sometimes more than the bride. Go back and show Nathalie how you look.'

There was just the slightest second of hesitation. And then Claudine walked out of the room.

'Well, you saved the day,' Lara commented. 'What I want to know is – why?'

'You think *I* want to end up being maid of honour?' Alice demanded. 'Come on, let's go. I wouldn't mind a glass of champagne right now.'

'I think you've earned it,' Lara agreed. 'And wait till you hear what I've just learned about dear Nathalie.'

Chapter Sixteen

Everyone staying at the château had gathered in a lovely panelled drawing room for drinks and appetizers. As Lara chatted with an aunt, Alice went over to Jack's father.

'Hello, Mr Baron, it's nice to see you again.'

The man looked at her vaguely.

'I'm Alice Henshaw, remember?'

'Of course,' he said quickly, though Alice seriously doubted it. 'How are you, my dear?'

'Very well, thank you.'

Jack and Nathalie joined them, and Jack spoke.

'Father, you haven't met my bride. This is Nathalie. Nathalie, I would like you to meet my father.'

Nathalie turned on the charm, just as she had with Jack's stepfather. 'Ah, monsieur, I am so very happy to meet my new *papa*!' She leaned forward to kiss his cheeks.

Mr Baron seemed a little taken aback. 'Yes, yes, delighted, delighted to meet you.'

Nathalie smiled prettily. 'And now, yes, I see well how Jack comes to be so handsome!'

Alice choked back a laugh. Lara was right – the girl certainly knew how to lie. With his bushy eyebrows, thick spectacles and unruly white hair, Mr Baron bore no resemblance at all to his son. He looked at Nathalie doubtfully and then turned to Jack, who just shrugged.

'And it is so very kind,' Nathalie went on, 'that you leave your estate to come to our marriage.'

The elderly man seemed completely bewildered. 'My estate?'

'She means the Hartfield Estate, where we used to live, Father. Nathalie, that's where I spent my childhood, but my father doesn't live there any more.'

'*Non?* Where do you live now?'

'I have rooms at the college where I teach,' he told her. 'Now that Jack doesn't live with me, I don't need very much space.'

Now it was Nathalie's turn to look puzzled. 'Rooms? How many rooms?'

'Two,' Mr Baron said. 'A sitting room and a bedroom.'

Nathalie seemed at a loss for words. Finally, she said, 'Well then, you do not need so many servants, do you?'

'Servants? There are no servants!'

'We've never had servants, Nathalie,' Jack said.

'But – at the estate . . . ?'

Jack rolled his eyes. 'We didn't live in a stately home, Nathalie. Hartfield Estate was a block of garden flats.'

'Garden flats,' Nathalie repeated.

'They were very nice flats,' Alice interjected. 'More like little houses. Two-up, two-down, right, Jack?'

'Exactly,' Jack said.

'Two up? I do not understand.'

'Two rooms upstairs, two rooms downstairs,' Jack explained.

'Four rooms,' Nathalie said faintly. 'That is all?'

'It was just the two of us,' Jack said. 'My father and me. We didn't need anything bigger.'

Nathalie looked as if she was having a hard time absorbing this information. She turned to Mr Baron.

'Perhaps you travel very much, monsieur? So you are not interested in keeping a large home?'

The man actually chuckled. 'You can't do much travelling on a schoolteacher's salary. Didn't Jack tell you that I'm a teacher?'

'Yes. I thought perhaps this amused you.'

'Well, I do enjoy my job. And it serves to pay the rent and bills.'

Slowly, Nathalie nodded.

'Of course, I go on holiday now and then. I go to the Lake District for a week every year.'

'Do you still stay at that little bed and breakfast?' Jack asked.

'Yes. It's a bit run-down now, but I'm used to it.'

'What means "run-down"?' Nathalie asked Alice in a whisper.

'Not in very good shape,' Alice said. 'Shabby. Jack, what's the word for 'shabby' in French?'

Jack used a word that made Nathalie go pale.

'And what do you plan to do when you finish university, son?'

'Nathalie and I will be moving back to England. I'll probably have to enrol in some courses so I can qualify to practise law there.'

Nathalie touched his arm. 'But, Jack . . . if there is no estate, how can we go back to England? Where will we live?'

'I'll see where I can take a course and we'll rent a bedsit nearby.'

'A bedsit?'

Alice explained. 'A room with a bed and a seating area. Like a studio.'

'But would it not be better to stay in Paris?' Nathalie

asked. 'We can live with your mother and Monsieur de Trouville.'

Jack shook his head so hard Alice was afraid he'd sprain his neck, and his eyes widened in horror.

'Forget it,' he declared sharply. 'There's no way I'll live with them.' His voice softened. 'It won't be for long,' he assured Nathalie. 'I'm sure I can finish any qualifying courses in a year. After that . . .'

'You will be a real lawyer,' Nathalie said, sounding a little brighter. 'We have house in London, yes?'

'Nathalie, do you have any idea what a London house costs? We won't be able to afford it.'

Nathalie's brow furrowed. 'But lawyers, they are very rich.'

'*Some* lawyers are,' Jack corrected her. 'The kind that go into corporate law. That's not what I want to do.' He turned back to his father. 'After I finish the courses, I'll have to get a trainee contract. I won't be making much money, but Nathalie and I should be able to rent a little flat. What do you think, Father?'

'Yes, yes, that sounds very nice,' he said vaguely. He'd clearly been distracted by a bookcase full of leather-bound volumes. 'Excuse me,' he murmured, and drifted over there.

Nathalie had turned even paler.

'You will excuse me, also,' she said. Stiffly, she walked towards the door.

Jack watched her leave the room. 'I hope she's not feeling ill. She was looking a bit sick.'

'I think that's pretty common,' Alice said. 'In her condition, I mean. By the way, I don't think I ever congratulated you. So . . . congratulations.'

She got a very brief and very small smile. 'Thanks.'

'You always said you wanted children.'

'Yeah. It's happening sooner than I expected, but . . .' He made a what-can-you-do gesture. 'As the French say, "*C'est la vie.*"'

'*C'est la vie,*' Alice echoed.

'You want children, don't you?' he asked suddenly.

She nodded. 'Of course. Not right now. But some day. At the right time. With the right person.'

He looked past her, and his eyes scanned the room. 'Where's Callum?'

'He left. We, um, had a long talk, and . . . and I don't think we'll be seeing much of each other any more.'

'Oh! I'm sorry to hear that. He seemed like a nice bloke.'

'He is. Just not the right bloke.'

Lara appeared by their side. 'Have either of you seen Harry?'

'He was here a few minutes ago,' Jack said.

'I can't find him anywhere,' she said.

'Maybe he's gone up to change for dinner,' Alice suggested.

Lara looked incredulous. 'Harry? Change for dinner?'

Christophe joined them. Having not noticed what he'd been wearing earlier, Alice had no idea if *he'd* changed for dinner but as usual, he looked extremely well groomed in his navy blazer and immaculately pressed trousers.

'There is the most beautiful sunset beginning,' he told them. 'Lara, *ma belle*, will you join me to watch it? Although, perhaps that is not to my advantage. How can I look at a sunset when I can look at you?'

No wonder Lara was so smitten, Alice thought. If a boy back home had ever said something like that to her, it would have made her gag. But with that French accent, the words sounded sincere and practically poetic. And Lara was only human. Alice watched the two walk off together and wondered if Harry stood a chance.

'Here come some friends from school,' Jack announced. Alice turned and saw a group of people in the doorway. 'Come and meet them,' Jack said as he started towards them.

'In a minute,' Alice said. She really wasn't in the mood

to be sociable. As soon as Jack's back was turned, she went the other way, to a door leading outside.

It *was* a pretty sunset, gold verging on orange. She spotted Lara and Christophe, and she headed in the opposite direction, towards the woods. She found a pathway, and took it. Surrounded by trees, she found the solitude and silence that she was craving.

At the same time, she felt unbearably lonely, and she almost wished she still had Callum there. But it had been the right thing to do. He had too many expectations of the relationship, and in her heart, she knew she'd never be able to love him the way he deserved to be loved. It was better to release him now, before they became even more entangled and it would be even harder to separate.

Now she had the freedom to put herself out there and hopefully meet someone else. Someone who could make her forget about Jack. Right now, she should go back to the party and meet those friends who'd just arrived from Paris. No, not right now. Later, when the sadness had passed. But she was beginning to wonder if that would ever happen. Her soulmate was getting married tomorrow, to a terrible girl he didn't even know. And even if he did learn that she'd been lying to him, what difference would it make? He was still going to marry her.

She continued to walk, and then, even though she couldn't see anyone, she heard a voice.

'What did you want to talk to me about?'

It was Harry's voice. Had Lara found him? She stepped away, not wanting to get any closer and disturb them. But then she heard another voice, and it wasn't Lara's. She stopped and listened.

'Oh, I just want to know you better. You are so very interesting to me.'

Nathalie.

'I'm interesting?'

Even without seeing Harry's face, Alice could imagine the bewilderment written all over it. She couldn't remember Nathalie paying any attention to Harry over the past couple of days.

'But of course! And you are so funny! Tell me about yourself.'

'There's not much to tell. I'm just a student.'

'*Non*, this is not true. I hear Lara say you are a duke.'

'Oh yeah, right. The duke of dorkdom.'

'And where is this place, dorkdom?'

There was a moment of silence.

'You're kidding, right?' Harry asked finally.

Nathalie's voice became softer, and Alice had to strain to hear her. She got the impression that the French girl had moved closer to Harry. 'What does this mean, kidding?'

Harry's voice changed too. Now he sounded flustered. 'Um, you know, I'm, uh, feeling a bit peckish.'

'Peckish?'

'Hungry. I think I'll go see if they've put out the buffet yet.'

'I come with you.'

Alice shrank back behind a tree and caught a glimpse of Harry and Nathalie moving down the path. Nathalie had put her arm through his.

Alice had to clap a hand over her mouth to keep from laughing. Unbelievable! Nathalie thought she'd found a better prospect than Jack. And this made perfectly good sense. Who would want to be the wife of a small-town solicitor when she could be the Duchess of Dorkdom?

It was starting to get dark, and she retraced her steps back towards the château. Once out of the woods, she saw that someone else had sought solitary refuge. Jack was sitting alone on a bench near the fountain.

Maybe she shouldn't bother him. But even as she was thinking this, she was making her way towards him.

His eyes were closed but he wasn't sleeping. There were creases on his forehead that made him look as if he was in pain.

'Jack? Are you OK?'

He opened his eyes. 'Oh, hi, Alice. I'm fine. Just a headache.'

'Want some company?'

He edged over to make room for her on the bench.

They sat in silence for a moment. But Jack kept giving her sidelong glances, and she had the feeling he wanted to talk. She knew him so well . . .

A memory came back. They were in their early teens, and he'd suddenly become moody, especially when they met just after school. She'd known something was bothering him, but every time she'd asked directly what was wrong, he'd say 'nothing'.

So she brought up random topics – lessons, homework, teachers, friends – and eventually he confessed that he was being bullied. *Then* they could talk openly about it, and work out how he would deal with it.

It was the same today, and she knew he wouldn't just tell her what was on his mind. She'd have to ease it out of him.

'So,' she began, 'you're getting married tomorrow. That's so amazing.'

'Yeah.'

'You must be feeling a bit anxious.'

'Why would I be anxious?' he asked sharply.

'Come on, Jack, I *know* you. You hate being in front of a crowd, having a load of people watching you. I remember the night before you had to give a speech in English. You were a nervous wreck!'

He grinned. 'I still don't like being the centre of attention, although training to be a lawyer pretty much cured me of nerves.'

'Maybe you're just nervous about the prospect of married life,' she said. 'Sharing a home with someone, being with that person all the time. You and Nathalie haven't been living together, have you?'

He shook his head.

'You don't even really know her all that well, do you?'

Again, he shook his head. But this time he offered more. 'We met at a party. She was cute, very flirty. We went out and she was fun. I was under a lot of pressure at uni, and she helped me take my mind off it.' He shifted uneasily in his seat. 'I think you can guess how we did that.'

'Just the one time?'

He nodded.

So Lara was right again.

'But you've spent more time together since . . .'

'After she gave me the news?' He smiled ruefully.

'And you got to know each other.'

'Not really. She knew I was from England, that my parents were divorced and my mother had married this boring French aristocrat, but that was about it.'

'And what did you learn about her?'

'Well, that she's a student too. Of course, we didn't have any classes together: she's studying French literature.'

Alice frowned but she didn't say anything.

'I knew she'd had a rough life,' he continued. 'She's dirt poor, you know. Works in the university canteen to pay her fees. Did I tell you she's an orphan?'

She's not an orphan, Jack, she wanted to say. She's not even a student. But what would be the point? 'Yes, you did.'

'I don't have much money, but I'm in better shape than she is. I'd buy her little things she admired – a piece of jewellery, a pair of shoes – and she'd be so thrilled, so grateful. But then she wanted more and more.' He grimaced. 'I had to borrow money from Christophe.'

She knew that couldn't have been easy for him. When they were young, Jack's father sometimes forgot to leave him his pocket money. Jack refused to take any money from her.

'Couldn't you just tell her you didn't have a lot of money?'

He shook his head. 'I felt like I had to keep giving her things, to make up for what I wasn't feeling.'

'You don't love her,' Alice whispered.

At first, she didn't think he'd heard her, and she was glad. But then he nodded.

'No.'

'Does she love you?'

'I don't see how she could. I wasn't much of a boyfriend. When I had a lot of work to do, I wouldn't see her for days. I wouldn't even call her. But when I did, she was never angry, she never berated me for ignoring her. She was always available. And we set the date. She wanted to get married before her pregnancy started to show.'

'That's understandable,' Alice said. 'It's hardly uncommon for a bride to be pregnant. But a lot of people still don't want the whole world to know.'

'I think she was more concerned about fitting into a nice dress.'

Alice couldn't help smiling. That sounded like Nathalie.

'No, I don't think she loves me,' Jack said abruptly. 'Any more than I love her.'

'Oh, Jack. I'm so sorry.'

'But I'm trying to be optimistic,' he said quickly. 'I know someone in law school: his parents are from Pakistan and they're very traditional. He was set up in an arranged marriage. He barely knew his wife when he married her. But they've been together for two years now, and he says they've grown to love each other.'

'Do you think that will happen with you and Nathalie?'

He turned to face her directly, and she was alarmed to see how misty his eyes were. He didn't say anything; he just stared at her, long and hard.

'Jack?'

He struggled to get some words out. And when he did, they weren't what she'd expected to hear.

'I – I've only ever loved one person.'

She didn't need to ask who that person was.

Almost unwillingly, he leaned towards her. It was as if some invisible force was pushing him, and he couldn't – or wouldn't – stop it. And then the same force began to push her.

Their lips met – and there it was again, that clearly remembered electric shock, the lightning strike. She pulled back.

'Jack, no! It isn't right!'

And before her emotions could stop her – before she

could kiss him the way she really wanted to kiss him, before she got in too deep – she stood up and ran back towards the château.

Chapter Seventeen

The sun had almost completely set, and the warmth of the day was gone. Lara hugged herself as they strolled around the château grounds.

'You are cold, *ma belle*?'

'A little,' Lara admitted.

Christophe slipped off his blue blazer and put it round Lara's shoulders.

'Now *you'll* be cold,' Lara told him.

In a softly seductive voice, he spoke in French. Lara thought she might have caught a word or two but they made no sense.

'Christophe, you know I can't understand you when you speak so fast.'

'I was quoting Baudelaire, a great French poet. I cannot communicate the true spirit of his words in English, but he speaks about the warm heart of one's beloved. I am trying to let you know that I cannot be cold in your presence.'

That was lovely, she thought. No one had ever quoted poetry to her before.

'You must improve your French, Lara,' he went on. 'There is so much great literature you would enjoy. It's truly a shame that you cannot comprehend it.'

'We've got great literature in Britain too,' she reminded him. 'Like Shakespeare.'

'Yes, yes, Shakespeare was a fine writer. But if you knew the literature of France, you would know true greatness.'

She didn't want to get into an argument over which country had the superior literary heritage. She was studying economics at uni, and she'd never been a big reader like Alice, so she wouldn't be able to provide much of a defence anyway.

'Shakespeare writes well of history,' Christophe continued. 'And his comedies are rather droll. But he cannot write of love.'

'What about *Romeo and Juliet*?'

He did his French shrug. 'Too adolescent.' He spoke again in French, and this time he was able to give her a more precise translation. '"Love is an ocean, and a woman is the shore." Victor Hugo.'

That was a familiar name. Then she remembered where she'd heard it before. '*Les Miserables*!'

'Precisely.'

She pursued this. 'You know, it's strange. I mentioned *Les Misérables* to Nathalie, and I couldn't remember the name of the author. She said it was Balzac.'

Christophe uttered a short laugh. 'No, I can't imagine that Nathalie would be able to answer a question like that.'

'She told me that was what she was reading at university, French literature.'

Christophe didn't say anything.

'She isn't really a student, is she? You said you knew her from your village. You must know that she's not an orphan, either.'

'How do you know these things?' Christophe asked sharply.

'Claudine told me.'

'Ah.'

'So why is she lying to Jack?'

He shrugged again. 'Perhaps to raise her station in life. What do you call it in Britain? Her class. So Jack would perceive her as having a similar social status to his own.'

'Jack doesn't care about social status,' Lara informed him.

'But Nathalie does not understand that. Here in France, an educated person would not be socially involved with a checkout girl.'

'I didn't know the French were so snobby.'

He looked at her with amusement. 'Are you telling me the English are so different?'

'Back home, a person's job doesn't put that person in a class,' she pointed out. 'Princess Diana was an aristocrat. But she worked as a nanny and a nursery teacher. Those aren't hoity-toity jobs.'

'Hoity-toity?'

'Upper class.'

'I see. Well, I can assure you, Nathalie is not of the upper class.'

'How do *you* know? Did you date her back in your village?' That would explain why Nathalie seemed to dislike him so much.

He was shocked by the notion. 'No, never!'

'Tell me what you know about her,' Lara demanded.

Suddenly, Christophe looked very nervous. His eyes darted around, as if he was afraid someone might be listening.

'Do you know her family?' Lara pressed.

He became very serious. 'If I tell you, you will not say you heard it from me.'

'Of course not.'

'Because she is very much ashamed,' he went on. 'Do you remember, when I asked about her family in the tea room? I was teasing her, because I knew she would not invite them. She was afraid I would reveal something of her background.'

'What *is* her background?' Images of petty thieves or drug dealers crossed Lara's mind.

'Her mother cleans my parents' home. Her father drives the local taxi.'

'What's wrong with that?'

'Well, it is not something one would want a prospective bridegroom from a better class to know.'

It was unbelievable, Lara thought. At the same time, it made sense. Nathalie wanted a husband who could provide her with a life of luxury. She took a job at a university where she could meet men with the potential to make a lot of money, or who came from well-off families. She made up a story to win their confidence and sympathy. And Jack fell for it.

Something else struck her. 'Wait a minute. You're Jack's friend. Why didn't you tell him about her?'

'In France, we do not interfere in relationships. Romance is sacred.'

'Oh, come on, Christophe. If I knew my friend was

being lied to, I'd tell her. That's what friends do.'

'Men are different, Lara.'

She frowned. She'd heard that before, she'd said it herself. It was true, in a way. Women talked much more openly about how they felt, they shared more with each other. Men held back. They thought it wasn't manly to talk about feelings. But there had to be a point where loyalty would rise above their macho standards.

'Jack's not rich, you know,' she said. 'He won't be able to give her a luxurious life.'

'Yes, I know that,' Christophe replied. 'And when she realizes that, the marriage will be over. After she has the baby, they will separate.'

'I'm not so sure about that,' Lara said sadly. 'Jack's parents were divorced when he was young. I think he would try very hard to keep his marriage together, for the sake of their child.'

'That's possible,' Christophe agreed. 'Perhaps he and Nathalie will simply take lovers. It is the French way.'

'Christophe! That's the kind of thing that happens in films. I don't think French people are so different from anyone else.'

He put an arm around her. 'My sweet, naive Lara. You will learn. We are not like you British.'

She stopped walking. 'What's that supposed to mean?'

'Your people are so prim and proper, so reserved. Your people are less enlightened in the ways of love; you cannot express yourselves. You have no passion.'

She might not have felt capable of arguing about literature, but she could certainly defend her nationality. 'That is such a stereotype!'

'There is often truth in stereotypes, Lara.'

'OK, we're probably more polite than the French are. We take our places in queues and we say "sorry" a lot. But we've got plenty of passion!'

'Really?' he said, with an expression that made it clear he highly doubted it.

She did the only thing she could think of to prove her point. Reaching up, she pulled him down towards her in an embrace, and kissed him with serious energy, only breaking away when she had to take a breath.

'There,' she said triumphantly. 'Do you still believe the English can't be passionate?'

'As I said before, Lara, I believe you have the heart of a Frenchwoman.'

The first time he'd said it, she'd been flattered. She was still sure he meant it as a compliment, she just wasn't so sure it felt like one.

There was something else, too. That kiss . . . obviously, she'd convinced him of her own ability to demonstrate passion. The only problem was – she hadn't *felt* the passion. This puzzled her. He was a good kisser – a very good kisser. Maybe she'd been too preoccupied to truly appreciate it. She couldn't stop thinking about her cousin who was about to marry a conniving, lying gold-digger.

'I suppose it doesn't matter whether Jack knows the truth about Nathalie,' she said. 'He'd still marry her.'

'Yes,' Christophe agreed. 'Jack is an honourable man.'

'Which, by the way, many believe to be a very British trait,' Lara noted.

'Let us not speak further of Jack and Nathalie,' Christophe said. 'I prefer to speak of us.'

'Us?'

'Yes. I am hoping you will come to visit me again soon.'

That was a relief. 'Of course! It's easy to hop over on the Eurostar. And you can visit me too.'

'Perhaps.' There was a distinct lack of enthusiasm in his tone. 'But I think France suits you far better than England suits me. And it would be a pleasure for you, yes? To get away from all that rain, the dreadful food . . .'

She immediately went on the defensive again. 'It doesn't rain *that* much. And for your information, you can eat very well in England.'

He continued as if she hadn't spoken. 'And you will get away from Englishmen.'

That stopped her in her tracks. 'What's wrong with Englishmen?'

'Surely I don't need to explain that to you.' Nevertheless, he went on to do so. 'Everyone knows about Englishmen. They're stuffy and repressed, and they make silly, vulgar jokes to deal with their own sexual inhibitions. They sit in pubs and drink warm beer and talk about football. And they have bad teeth.'

'That's ridiculous!' Lara exclaimed. 'How many Englishmen have you ever really known?'

'Take your friend Harry, for example . . .'

Lara interrupted. 'Just stop right there. Yes, Harry likes pubs, and OK, the beer isn't very cold. And yeah, he likes his football. But he's not stuffy or repressed. And his teeth are perfectly fine.'

'What about his terrible jokes?'

'They're not always terrible. He can be quite funny sometimes.'

Christophe spoke kindly. 'He is vulgar, Lara.'

'Don't you dare talk like that about him! You don't even know Harry!'

Christophe was clearly startled by the sharpness of her response. 'But you are so far above him, Lara. He's not right for a girl like you.'

She brushed that aside. 'And I'll tell you something

else about Harry. If he thought a friend of his was being lied to by the woman he was about to marry, he'd tell him. Whether it made any difference or not.'

Christophe shook his head. 'I cannot tell Jack about Nathalie.'

'But I still don't understand why! And don't tell me French attitudes are that different from British. I just don't buy it.'

Christophe looked pained. 'Could we please speak of something else?'

But Lara hadn't finished. 'And if you're not going to tell Jack, then I will.'

Now Christophe looked frightened. 'But you cannot! Nathalie will think you learned it from me.'

'So what if I did?'

Christophe bit his lip nervously. 'Then Nathalie will tell something about me.'

Lara raised her eyebrows. 'You have secrets, Christophe?'

He looked around again, and lowered his voice. 'You say you have no interest in social class. So I will tell you. But you must swear to me that you will never repeat what I am about to tell you.'

Lara looked at him in alarm. 'Good grief, Christophe! What are you going to tell me? Are you a criminal?'

He took a deep breath. 'My name, Lara . . . what you

call the surname . . . is not de la Martinet. It is Martin.'

'Martin,' Lara repeated, saying it as he had said it, the French way, with the accent on the second syllable. 'OK. So what?'

'It is one of the most common, ordinary names in France.'

'OK,' she said again. 'I still don't get it.'

'I do not have an aristocratic heritage. My parents are lower class. They come from the same background as Nathalie.'

'But . . . you said her mother works for your family. Jack said you live in a posh flat. And I've seen how you throw money around: you're obviously not poor.' A thought struck her, and she gasped. 'Ohmigod, Christophe. Are you, like, a drug dealer or something?'

He shook his head. And in a voice that resonated with shame, he said, 'My parents won the Lotto.'

'Well . . . that's great. You're very lucky. Why does it have to be such a secret? Are you afraid people will ask you for money?'

'Lara, you don't understand. I have worked very hard to present myself in the best possible light. As Christophe de la Martinet, I have stature, prestige. Money cannot buy this. And you see, when I made the comment about Nathalie's parents at the tea room, later she threatened me. She said that if I reveal to Jack the truth about her, she will let people at the university know about my background. I will be ruined.'

Lara's mouth fell open. 'You can't be serious. People care that much about family?'

'Well . . . the right people do. The society in which I belong.'

She burst out laughing. He was just as bad as Nathalie.

'I don't belong to that kind of society, Christophe.'

'It does not matter so much for a woman. She can rise in society through the man she is with. Just as Nathalie will do with Jack.'

Lara closed her eyes. 'Christophe . . . that's just plain sick.'

'Please, Lara, let us not argue,' he said smoothly. 'It is a beautiful night, we are walking under the stars. We will speak no more of these things. We will speak only of love.' He put an arm round her.

She was no longer in the mood for that kind of talk either, and she eased herself out from under his arm. 'Actually, I'd rather go back to the château. The food must be out now and I'm hungry. Aren't you?'

'I am hungry for you, Lara.' He spoke softly, seductively.

'That's nice,' she said. 'But I'm hungry for food.'

He looked at her reprovingly. 'A French girl would never think of food at a moment like this.'

'Sorry, Christophe,' she said lightly. 'I guess I'm still pretty English that way.'

'Lara! I am shocked.'

'That I'm still English?'

But he actually looked seriously distressed. 'Now that you know I am not an aristocrat, you are no longer interested in me.'

'No, it's not that at all, Christophe. It's because you care about it. That's why I'm not interested.'

He looked confused. She would have explained, but he was distracted by the appearance of two girls coming along the path, chatting in French. Friends of Jack's probably, Lara thought.

'Christophe!' one of them called.

He brightened. 'Elodie! *Comment ça va, ma belle?*'

Lara turned and started down the path. She hadn't made it very far before she heard Christophe's call.

'Lara!'

She turned.

'My jacket?'

She slipped off the jacket and held it out for him. He retrieved it with a brief '*merci*' and went back to join the two French girls.

Back in the panelled drawing room, the crowd had grown. People were filling their plates from a buffet table that had been set up, but Harry wasn't among them. Lara spotted Jack, talking in French with people she didn't know, but she didn't see Nathalie. Or Alice either. She took some cold meat and salads from the buffet and looked around for a place to sit and eat. She didn't particularly want to join her relatives, but she didn't want to pretend she could speak French with Jack's friends.

Finally, plate in hand, she left the room and went in search of Alice. There was that bench outside that she liked, the one that was hidden from view by the big fountain. Balancing the plate, she moved around the fountain and found that the bench *was* occupied – but not by Alice.

Harry sat there by himself. He practically jumped when he heard her approach, but relaxed when he saw it was her.

'Hi,' he said.

'Can I join you?'

'Suit yourself.'

It wasn't much of an invitation, but she couldn't blame him for acting a bit cold. She hadn't been paying much attention to him lately.

They sat in silence while they ate. Lara tried to come up with a topic that didn't involve their relationship.

'Cal left,' she said finally. 'He and Alice broke up.'

'Yeah, I know.'

There was another silence.

'What are you doing out here by yourself?' she asked.

'Hiding.'

She bit her lip. 'From who? Me?'

'Ha! Don't flatter yourself. What are *you* doing all alone? Where's your new boyfriend?'

She supposed she could have gone all innocent and pretended she didn't know who he was referring to, but what was the point?

'He's a jerk,' she said.

He sniffed. 'I could have told you that a while back.'

'You didn't answer my question,' she said. 'Who are you hiding from?'

He hesitated.

'Let me guess,' she went on. 'One of the hot French girls is coming on to you.'

'Close,' he said.

'What do you mean, "close"?'

He gave a nonchalant shrug. 'I wouldn't really call her "hot".'

241

She raised her eyebrows. 'Who are you talking about?'

An oddly abashed grin appeared briefly. 'Nathalie.'

'*What?*'

He shook his head ruefully. 'It was the weirdest thing. Out of the blue, she came up to me and said she had to talk to me. She dragged me out into the woods and started giving me all this crap about how she found me so interesting and funny, and how she wanted to get to know me better. She said she'd been watching me ever since we arrived and she couldn't stop thinking about me.'

Lara stared at him. 'You're kidding me, right?'

'Nope.'

Lara shook her head in disbelief. 'Wow. She is one weird girl.'

'Why do you say that?' Harry challenged her. 'Because she thinks I'm fit?'

'Because she's getting married tomorrow! And girls who are getting married don't usually run around the night before flirting with other guys.'

Harry relented. 'She *is* strange.'

'That's putting it mildly.' Lara proceeded to tell Harry what she'd learned from Claudine and Christophe. The secrets were so ridiculous, she didn't care about revealing them.

Harry was aghast. 'You mean she's been lying to Jack all this time?'

'Yep. She's only marrying him to raise her social status. She thinks Jack's rich.'

'Why would she think that?'

'Because his mother's married to a rich man?'

'And Christophe isn't telling Jack about this because . . . ?'

'Because Nathalie will ruin him by telling everyone he won the lottery!'

'Jeez,' Harry groaned. 'What a couple of losers.'

'Plus, Christophe says guys don't talk about their relationships with each other.'

Harry grimaced. 'Maybe. But when I get back home, the first thing I'm going to do is call Cal and see how he's doing.'

She wasn't surprised. Harry was the kind of guy who cared about people. It was one of the things that had attracted her to him in the first place.

'Are you going to tell Jack about Nathalie?' he asked.

'It's too late now,' she replied. 'He'll marry her anyway – she's pregnant.'

Harry whistled. 'Which makes her flirting with me even weirder. Hey, you know what she asked me? "Where is Dorkdom"?'

'Huh?'

'Remember back when we first met her? When she said I had the same first name as Prince Harry?'

'That's right. I told her you were the "Duke of Dorkdom".' Lara drew in her breath. 'You don't think she really believes you're a duke?'

'That would explain the flirting,' Harry said. 'And don't forget Jack's last name. Maybe she thinks he's a baron.'

'She can't be that stupid,' Lara declared.

Harry grinned. 'She was coming on to *me*. She can't be that bright.'

'Stop that,' Lara said. 'Even if she didn't think you're a duke, why wouldn't she flirt with you? *I* did.'

'That's true,' Harry admitted. 'In fact, if memory serves, you came on to me first.'

'That's right.' She flashed back to that first day at uni. 'There was some guy sitting by you and he was freaking out because the textbook he needed wasn't in the library. And you offered to let him use yours. I remember thinking, what a nice guy he is.'

'Oh yeah? I thought you just wanted to borrow the book too.'

She smiled. 'Well, there *was* that.'

He smiled back. 'So you admit that it's just possible Nathalie was into me?'

She nodded. 'Very possible. And if she was even remotely desirable, I'd be jealous.'

'What about your Frenchman?'

She cocked her head thoughtfully. 'Once, when I was about five years old, I was with my mother in a department store at Christmas time. There was this huge Christmas tree on display, all decorated and lit up, and under the tree there were the most gorgeously wrapped packages I'd ever seen. There was one in particular that I couldn't take my eyes off. I can see it now like it was yesterday. It was wrapped in shiny gold paper and had a huge red bow.'

'What does this have to do with the Frenchman?'

'When no one was looking, I got down on the floor. I pulled off the red ribbon and I tore off the gold paper, and then I opened the box. And do you know what was inside?'

'What?'

'Nothing. It was empty. Because it was just a prop.' She paused. 'That was Christophe.'

Harry got it.

'But you,' Lara continued. 'You're the big, beautiful teddy bear, sitting under the Christmas tree waiting for me. You don't need any wrapping.'

She edged closer, and so did he, and they put their

arms around each other. She was almost grateful to Christophe for having kissed her earlier. Now she had something to compare it with. And she could fully appreciate the electricity that shot through her, the sense of wanting to never let go. *This* was passion.

Unfortunately, Harry hadn't taken his plate of food from his knees, and their movement sent the contents of his dinner all over his jeans.

'Oops! I'm sorry,' Lara exclaimed.

Harry surveyed the damage. 'I'm not. Now I've got jeans with souvenirs.'

'Go back to the buffet and get more food,' Lara instructed him. 'I'm going to run up to my room and find a jumper. It's really getting cold.'

'You could have my jacket,' Harry offered.

'But then *you'd* be cold.'

'That's true,' Harry said. 'Yeah, go and get a jumper.'

She grinned, planted another kiss on his lips and ran back inside.

She found Alice in their room, already in her pyjamas, lying on her bed and staring at the ceiling.

'What's the matter? Aren't you feeling well?' Lara asked.

When Alice didn't answer, Lara sat down on the edge of the bed and waited. Finally, Alice spoke.

'Jack and I . . . we kissed.'

Lara took her hand. 'Oh, Alice.'

'And I pushed him away.'

'That can't have been easy.'

'It wasn't. But I had to, Lara. Because it was wrong. He's getting married tomorrow.'

'I know.' Lara squeezed her hand. 'Damn, it's so unfair!'

Alice sat up. 'Why aren't you with Christophe?'

'He's a jerk too,' Lara said. 'Long story. I'll tell you about it tomorrow. Harry's waiting for me outside.' She considered telling Alice about Nathalie's overtures to Harry, but decided it could wait. There was no point in giving Alice more reasons to feel awful about this marriage.

Alice smiled. 'I'm glad. You two belong together.'

'You look exhausted,' Lara said. 'I'll just grab my jumper and let you sleep.'

Obediently, Alice closed her eyes. Lara picked up the jumper and left the room. Then she decided to use the toilet before going back outside. Hopefully, she and Harry would have more time for cuddling, and she wanted to be comfortable.

She'd just closed the cubicle door in the Ladies when she heard someone else come in. Peeking through the thin gap between the door and the wall, she saw Nathalie walking across the room. She paused in front of the mirror for a moment of self-admiration, and then went to the dispensing machine on the wall.

She put some coins in the slot. Lara couldn't see what button she pushed but she saw what came out of the machine. A slim, white, paper-wrapped tube.

Lara put a hand to her mouth and muffled an automatic gasp. She continued to watch until Nathalie went into a cubicle. She debated making a run for it, but there was the possibility that Nathalie might be watching from *her* gap. So she held her breath and waited.

Nathalie only took a minute but it felt like an eternity. Finally, Lara heard the toilet flush, and the sound of the door being unlocked. She heard Nathalie's stilettos click-clacking on the floor as she made her way to the exit. And she heard something else.

Nathalie was *humming*. The tune was familiar – it was probably some current pop hit. It was light and cheerful, the kind of tune someone who didn't have any particular cares would hum.

Lara waited another minute, to avoid running into Nathalie in the corridor. Then she sped out of the Ladies and back to her room.

Alice hadn't fallen asleep yet. She opened her eyes when Lara entered.

'I was just thinking,' Alice said sleepily. 'I wonder if she knows for sure that it's *Jack's* baby.'

Lara sat down on the bed.

'I was just thinking,' she said, 'that maybe there isn't a baby at all.'

Chapter Eighteen

On the morning of the marriage of Jack Baron and Nathalie Dupont, Alice was trying to figure out how to stop it.

Harry didn't understand why it was a tricky situation. 'Lara just tells him what she saw last night. She's not pregnant so he doesn't have to marry her. That's all there is to it.'

Alice shook her head. 'It's not that easy. I'm sure he sees the engagement as a promise. He asked her to marry him and now he has to do it.'

Lara agreed. 'You don't really know Jack, Harry. He's so honourable it's infuriating.' She proudly added, 'My cousin may be half French, but he's still an Englishman at heart.'

'I'm sure there are honourable Frenchmen too,' Alice chided her.

'Possibly,' Lara acknowledged. 'I just haven't met any lately.'

'So if you're not going to tell him, how are you going to stop him from making the biggest mistake of his life?' Harry wanted to know.

'I'm thinking, I'm thinking,' Alice replied.

'Well, you don't have much time,' Harry warned her. He checked his watch. 'The wedding's in three hours.'

They left the room and started down the stairs. 'It's funny,' Harry mused. 'I've heard of brides who don't want people to know they're pregnant when they get married. Here's a bride who doesn't want anyone to know she's *not* pregnant!'

They were rounding the corner on the stairway as he spoke, and Alice caught her breath. The maid of honour was at the foot of the stairs. How much had she heard?

Claudine said: 'I hear you say "pregnant!" You know!'

'We know what?' Lara asked cautiously.

Claudine lowered her voice and spoke conspiratorially. 'Nathalie and Jack, they are having a baby! It is big secret. Of course, Jack, he knows. But you will not tell?'

Alice smiled. 'Claudine, I can safely promise you, we will tell no one that Nathalie is pregnant.'

'I think maybe she will ask me to be godmother,' Claudine confided before scampering off.

'Maybe we should warn her not to start knitting bootees just yet,' Lara murmured.

'So even her best friend doesn't know,' Harry remarked. 'I'll say this for Nathalie. She knows how to keep a secret.'

The dining room didn't appear to be open for business that morning. The tables where they'd been eating had disappeared, and there was no breakfast laid out on the sideboard.

Harry was extremely dismayed. 'What's going on?' he demanded.

He got his answer immediately. Madame de Trouville entered the room, followed by four men. Three were carrying boxes and the fourth wheeled an enormous cart.

'Is that breakfast?' Harry asked hopefully.

'We will be using this room for the pre-wedding reception,' Jack's mother told them. 'These people are from the catering company.'

Alice was surprised. 'There's a reception *before* the wedding?'

'But of course, my dear. When guests begin to arrive, they will be shown in here for champagne and *les hors d'oeuvres*.'

'Starters,' Lara translated for Harry.

'Then, when it is time for the ceremony, they will be

252

directed to the grand ballroom. Following the ceremony, the wedding reception will be held outside in the marquee. Would one of you look out there and see if the workers have put it up?'

Alice went to the windows, pulled back the curtains, and saw that the château grounds were in the process of transformation. An enormous white marquee was being erected by half a dozen men in overalls. More men were in the trees that encircled the area, stringing what looked like fairy lights. A woman passed across the lawn with a cart laden with floral centrepieces. It was going to be quite an occasion.

Lara joined her by the window. 'While people are eating in the marquee, the ballroom will be cleared for dancing afterwards.'

'I didn't realize it was going to be so grand,' Alice said. Her stomach was churning, and it wasn't from hunger. Did she really have the nerve to disrupt this extravaganza?

Jack's mother overheard her. 'This is my only child, and his poor bride has no one to provide a decent wedding for her.'

Lara and Alice exchanged looks.

'And my husband and I have some important acquaintances coming to the wedding,' Madame de Trouville went on to say. 'People who will expect an impressive *fête*, and we are socially obligated to present a classic and refined occasion. Everything must be absolutely perfect. I don't want any surprises.' She said this with a strong emphasis, as if she half expected one of them to disrupt the event.

Alice smiled thinly. 'Where are the bride and groom?'

'Nathalie will be staying in her room until the ceremony,' the woman informed her. 'The hairdresser and make-up consultant arrive shortly. Jack is playing tennis with his best man.'

'On his wedding day?' Harry asked in disbelief.

But Alice just smiled. Tennis . . . Jack's special method of stress relief. It took his mind off any problem or situation he was about to encounter. She could see him now, running, sweating, chasing the ball, trying desperately to drive this imminent disaster out of his mind. She wished she could be with him right that minute, to comfort him and tell him it was going to be all right, that she would save him. As soon as she figured out how to do it.

'I'm hungry,' Harry said plaintively.

'Breakfast is being served in the sitting room,' Jack's mother informed him. Then she turned to the people who were laying a cloth on the long buffet table, let out a horrified gasp and spoke sharply in French.

'What's wrong?' Alice asked.

'I specifically ordered linen for the tablecloths. That looks like cotton!' She stormed over to the team of caterers.

'Let's get out of here,' Lara whispered. 'She scares me.'

They went to the sitting room, where Harry breathed a sigh of relief. A table had been filled with baskets of breads, a bowl of fruit, coffee and fruit juice.

'I don't think I can eat,' Alice told Lara. 'My stomach's in knots.'

'You *have* to eat.' Lara's voice was firm. 'You're going to need your strength.'

'For what?'

'A battle like this cannot be fought on an empty stomach. Harry, are all those croissants for you alone?' Lara stared at his overflowing plate.

'I need sustenance,' Harry replied. 'This has been a very stressful weekend. I still can't believe the bride came on to me last night.'

He spoke with righteous indignation, but Alice had to smile at the hint of pride in his voice. And it was just then that the germ of an idea took root.

'And I can't believe his best man didn't tell him about her,' Harry continued. 'These people don't know the meaning of friendship.'

They sat down at a table.

'Harry, are you angry at me?' Alice asked suddenly.

'What?'

'Because of Cal. Are you cross?'

Harry shook his head. 'I feel sorry for him, but better to end it now before you're in too deep. Nah, I'm not angry at you.'

'Good,' Alice said. 'Because I'm going to need you to make this wedding not happen.'

'You've got a plan?' Lara asked excitedly.

'Something's brewing.'

'How about this?' Lara said. 'When the judge or whoever he is asks if anyone present can show just cause why this marriage shouldn't take place, you stand up and say something.'

'No, too *EastEnders*. This is better.'

'What I don't understand,' Harry said, 'is why she still wants to marry him. She must have realized by now that he's not rich. And if she's not pregnant – well, I just don't get it.'

'I guess she figures anything is better than going back to her old job,' Lara said. 'And at least she gets to be a princess for a day, with a tiara and everything.'

Harry took another pastry from the bread basket and bit into it with gusto. Crumbs landed all over his T-shirt but his eyes lit up in delight.

Alice studied him thoughtfully. 'Princess for a day . . . yeah, that's pretty good. But maybe she'd rather be duchess for a lifetime.'

'What are you talking about?' Lara asked.

'She thinks Harry's a duke, right?'

Lara nodded. 'The Duke of Dorkdom.'

'Harry, did you tell her the truth?'

Harry started on another chocolate croissant. 'I told her I was kidding, but she didn't know what the word meant. And I didn't tell her.'

'Excellent.' Alice smiled. 'This really might work.' She began to explain.

It was an outrageous idea, totally crazy, and personally, Alice had to doubt her own sanity in coming up with it. Lara reacted as if her friend had just lost her mind. Harry was so confounded he stopped eating.

But at this point in time, with so much at stake, she was ready to try anything to stop the love of her life from marrying another woman.

Chapter Nineteen

Alice studied herself in the mirror. In all modesty, she had to admit that she looked as good as she ever had. When she'd chosen the slinky sky-blue dress, she'd worried that it might be a bit too low-cut for a day wedding, and she'd packed a little cream-coloured camisole to wear under it. But she'd decided to go without it – today, she wanted to look as desirable as possible. And her simple beige straw hat would add a ladylike touch.

She tried to see herself as Jack would see her. Old friend, childhood sweetheart? Or the girl he wished was standing by his side at the altar? Or whatever it was that a bride and groom stood in front of when they got married in a château.

Carefully, she dabbed some pale-blue eye shadow on her lids, and then went to work on her eyelashes. She'd borrowed Lara's waterproof mascara for this – she didn't want any rivers of black dripping down her face during the ceremony.

But if all worked according to plan, she wouldn't be shedding any tears – unless they were tears of triumph.

She was applying a pink lipstick when Lara came into the Ladies. She was in her wedding finery too, a pale-yellow sheath with long sheer sleeves.

'You're absolutely gorgeous,' she told Alice.

'You too,' Alice automatically responded. 'Lara, my plan – do you think it's totally insane?'

'Yes,' Lara replied promptly. 'But that doesn't mean it can't work.'

'It's all up to Harry, really, isn't it? Do you think he's up to it?'

'Yes,' Lara said, and there was no mistaking the pride in her voice. 'You know, it's ironic. All this time, I've been complaining that Harry doesn't appreciate me. And now I'm beginning to realize that all this time, it's me who didn't appreciate Harry.'

Alice hugged her friend. 'I'm so happy you two are back together.'

'Me too,' Lara said. 'But I'll be even happier if – I mean, *when* – you and Jack are back together too.'

Her confidence was contagious. Alice tossed her make-up bag back into her clutch. 'I'm going to look at the ballroom, do some reconnaissance.'

'Check out the marquee too,' Lara advised. 'Because if all goes according to plan, we may never get inside it.'

Alice was walking down the stairs when she encountered Madame de Trouville. 'Ah, my dear, I could use your help right now. Nathalie needs help with her zip and I don't have my glasses with me.'

What could she say? Reluctantly, she followed Jack's mother into the room where Jack and Nathalie had been staying.

The beautiful room was in a state of chaos. Items of clothing were strewn everywhere, along with the remnants of breakfast on trays. A hairdryer, various-sized brushes and bottles were all over the dressing table as the hairdresser made valiant attempts to create something elegant with Claudine's wild red hair.

But Alice's eyes were on the bride.

'You look beautiful,' she blurted out. As much as Alice disliked the girl, she had to admit that. The white gown wasn't one of those puffy meringue dresses – it was simple and sleek and clearly expensive. It had tiny lace cap sleeves and delicately appliquéd lace at the waist. Nathalie's hair had been styled behind her ears, to allow the veil to hang well. When she saw Alice, she lifted it.

'You will do zip?'

Alice nodded and approached. How easy it would be, she thought, to jiggle the zip a bit, pull a little too hard, get it caught in the fabric . . .

But she didn't. She zipped up the dress, fastened the little hook at the top, and stepped back. Nathalie examined herself in the mirror.

'Yes,' she said with satisfaction. 'Perfect.'

'But you are missing something,' Claudine called out.

A conscience, maybe? thought Alice.

Jack's mother returned, and in her hands she held the missing item. It was a nice tiara, Alice thought. Not too gaudy or extravagant. Crystals and pearls were entwined in an intricate design in the gold-coloured metal.

'Ooh, it sparkles!' Claudine enthused.

'Eighteen-carat gold,' Madame de Trouville announced. She indicated the smaller brilliant gems. 'And these are diamonds, not crystals.'

She placed it carefully over the veil and secured it with pins. Nathalie immediately began to rearrange it, and Jack's mother wrung her hands.

'Please, my dear! You must be very careful with the tiara,' she begged her. 'It's quite valuable. It belonged to my husband's mother, and he intends to give it to his daughter when she marries. He didn't want me to offer it, but I told him, every bride deserves a tiara.' She added another pin to Nathalie's hair.

'There! You look lovely.' She turned to Alice. 'Don't you think so?'

'Yes, lovely.' But as far as Alice was concerned, there was still something missing. In her experience, brides looked happy. Even if they were nervous or tense, they were smiling.

Nathalie didn't smile. And her blue eyes were blank. She didn't look nervous, or excited, or apprehensive . . . in fact, the only word Alice could think of to describe her expression was – bored. She felt herself shudder. It was all so depressing – a bride who lied about a pregnancy to marry someone she didn't even love. And a groom who was trying to do the right thing.

But she refused to let a cloud of gloom settle on her. There was too much at stake.

She backed out of the room. 'Excuse me, I've got things to do,' she blurted and fled.

Guests had begun to arrive. Alice caught a glimpse of men in suits and women in elegant attire entering the château. Christophe was at the door to greet them and usher them into the dining room where the pre-ceremony reception would take place. Briefly, she considered stopping there herself, for a quick gulp of courage-inducing champagne. But she needed to keep her wits about her so she headed directly to the grand ballroom.

It was all set up for the ceremony. About a hundred chairs covered with white cloths were set up in rows on either side of an aisle. A red carpet covered the aisle. At the front of the room was a podium, and huge bouquets of red and white roses rested on either side of it.

From there, she went outside. Workers were still putting pegs in the ground to secure the tent from any gusts of wind. Alice looked through one of the open flaps, and saw long tables set with glasses and silverware. In the centre of the room, on a pedestal, rested the wedding cake.

She moved in closer to get a good look. It wasn't like any wedding cake she'd ever seen before – no white icing, no fancy flowers made of marzipan, no plastic bride and groom on top. It wasn't even an actual cake. What looked like hundreds of pastry balls had been stacked in tiers, rising like a pyramid.

'It's traditional for French weddings,' said a voice from behind her. She turned and faced Jack.

He looked incredibly handsome in his black suit, white shirt and white tie. His hair was still wet from the shower and she could see the ridges made by a comb.

He looked calm – no, not calm. Resigned.

'It's called a croquembouche. Cream-filled pastry puffs covered with a caramel sugar glaze.'

'Sounds delicious,' Alice said.

'It is. Better than our wedding cakes, I think. Ours look prettier, but these are tastier.' He gave her a slight smile. 'Some things are better in France.'

'How do you feel? Are you nervous?'

The smile vanished. 'I feel . . . I feel like I've screwed up my life.'

'No, that's not true,' Alice said. 'You're finishing university, you're going to be a lawyer. You're coming back to England to be a solicitor. It's everything you've ever wanted.'

'Not everything,' he replied. Then, suddenly, he asked, 'Why did we lose touch, Alice?'

It wasn't the time to remind him that it was his decision. 'I don't know,' she said instead. 'It's what happens, I guess, when people move on with their lives.'

'It was a mistake,' he said.

She nodded. 'I know.'

'You feel the same way?'

'Yes. I do.' Then she felt her cheeks grow red. 'I do' was what brides and grooms said.

'Everything could have been so different,' he said softly.

It was strange – there were people all around, setting the tables, adjusting chairs – but from the way they were talking, they could have been all alone. She could feel tears burning in the back of her eyes. Fiercely, she fought them back. She wanted desperately to tell him – we've got a plan, this doesn't need to happen, you don't have to marry her.

But all she could say was, 'Maybe it's not the end of the world, Jack.'

Could she see a glimmer of hope in his eyes? Or maybe he was just seeing the hope in hers. There wasn't much time to contemplate this. Christophe came into the marquee.

'There you are!' he said to Jack. 'People are arriving and you should be at the door to greet them.'

Abruptly, Jack turned away from her and walked out of the marquee. A moment later, Alice followed. She went back into the château and made her way to the room for the pre-wedding reception.

French conversation filled the air as the dressed-up men and women took glasses of champagne and canapés from waiters who moved around the room with trays held high. Alice accepted a glass of champagne and went to a corner of the room where she waited for Harry and Lara.

More people came. Monsieur and Madame de Trouville made a grand entrance. She supposed Jack's father should have been there too, but he was probably hiding somewhere with a book. She saw Jack come in with Christophe, and they started making the rounds, shaking hands, kissing women on their cheeks.

Nathalie wasn't there, of course. She'd make *her* grand entrance in the ballroom. Alice checked her watch. The ceremony would begin in less than an hour.

She downed her champagne. It was probably a stupid thing to do – she'd barely eaten anything at breakfast, so she was already feeling light-headed. Not sick, though. In fact, she felt better. Braver. Which was one of the dangers of drinking, she knew that. It made you think you could do things you couldn't, or shouldn't.

Well, she wasn't about to drive a car or take an exam. And at this point, the chief responsibility for carrying out the plan lay with Harry. And if it didn't work – at least she could run back to her room and cry herself to sleep.

Lara and Harry arrived and came directly to her. They didn't even take a glass of champagne, though Harry did manage to snatch a couple of goodies from a waiter's tray.

'Are you ready?' Lara asked.

Alice nodded. 'And you?' she asked Harry.

'I wish there was a beer around here,' he grumbled.

Lara rolled her eyes. 'If you do this right, I'll treat you to beer for six months.'

'A year,' Harry said.

'Done.'

Alice checked her watch. 'OK, it's time. You know where the room is?'

Harry left, and Alice whispered to Lara. 'How long do you think it will take him?'

'Let's give him ten minutes. He's not a fast talker.'

It was the longest ten minutes Alice had ever waited, and she was sorely tempted to take another champagne, but she really needed to stay alert. The timing was essential. Some of the guests had begun leaving the room, and she knew they were heading for the ballroom. Despite the champagne, she started to feel nervous.

She took a deep breath and checked her watch. 'OK. Let's do it.'

Together, she and Lara approached Jack. He was engaged in conversation with some older people, probably friends of his mother's and stepfather's. Alice hung back while Lara touched his arm, and he turned.

'Jack, I need to show you something. Could you come with me?'

'Lara, I can't leave now, the ceremony's about to start.'

'It's important, Jack.'

Alice stepped forward. 'Very important.'

Puzzled, he looked at her. Then he turned back to the people he'd been talking to. 'Excuse me for a moment.'

He followed Alice and Lara out of the room. 'What's going on?' he asked.

'You need to see this,' Alice said.

'I need to see *what*?' He was beginning to sound annoyed. Alice was starting to feel sick – but maybe that was just the champagne.

They went to the door of the bridal suite. Harry had followed Lara's orders – the door wasn't completely closed.

'What are you doing?' Jack asked. 'She's getting ready. And I'm not supposed to see her till she comes down the aisle. Isn't that the rule?'

Alice put a finger to her lips, and gave the door a slight shove, just enough so they could all hear the conversation going on inside.

'You have a château?' Nathalie was asking.

They heard Harry's voice. 'It's not a *large* castle. Dorkdom isn't one of the great titles, like York or Lancaster. My staff is small.'

'You have servants?'

'Just the usual. A butler, a housekeeper, a cook. Maids

and footmen, of course. A valet and a chauffeur. If I had a wife, I would hire a lady's maid, of course. But unfortunately, I live there alone.'

'But your little friend, Lara?'

'Oh, she's a lot of fun. But the woman who marries me will be a duchess. I don't think Lara's cut out for that.'

'I understand,' Nathalie said. 'She has no elegance.'

'Too true.'

Out in the hall, Lara made the gesture of wringing someone's neck, and Alice wasn't sure whose.

'I wish I could meet someone like you,' Harry said.

'Someone *like* me?' Nathalie asked. There was a moment of silence. 'What about – me?'

'It's a little late for that,' Harry said. 'You're getting married in fifteen minutes.'

'Fifteen minutes,' Nathalie said. 'That is enough time for me to escape.'

'Escape?'

'I do not want to marry Jack. He is a nothing, a nobody! We call a taxi, we go to the train station. You take me to your castle in England and I will be your duchess.'

'Are you serious?'

'*Oui!* Go now, quickly, and call a taxi. I will change my dress.'

'But what about Jack?'

Out in the hall, Alice looked at him.

'Yes, what about Jack?' she asked quietly.

Jack pushed the door and it swung completely open. Harry stepped back and put up his hands in an exaggerated position of self-defence. Nathalie's expression was unreadable.

She spoke in French. And Alice didn't even need Lara's excited translation to understand what Nathalie was telling Jack.

'She wants out! She's leaving him for Harry!'

Jack's face was a mask of confusion. 'But – but what about our baby?' he asked in English.

Nathalie switched to English. 'There is no baby, Jack. I was never pregnant. Now, I go with Harry.'

Lara stepped forward. 'Just hold on one minute, Nathalie. That's my boyfriend you're talking about.'

Nathalie smirked. 'Harry say you cannot be a duchess.'

'He's right,' Lara agreed. 'He can't make me a duchess because he's not a duke.'

'What?' She turned to Harry. 'I do not understand.'

Harry looked down, as if he was ashamed and couldn't meet her eyes. For a man with no dramatic skills, he was actually doing a pretty decent job of it. 'I am so in love with you, Nathalie. I was trying to impress you, so you wouldn't marry Jack. But now I must confess – I'm not really a duke. But if you love me as I love you, this won't matter, will it?'

'You – you have no château?'

Harry shook his head. 'Sorry, my dear, darling Nathalie. But I have some pretty decent student digs back home. You're welcome to live with me there. I don't have much money, but we'll live on love. OK?'

Nathalie stared at him in horror.

'Shall I translate that into French, Nathalie?' Jack asked.

Clearly, that wasn't necessary. Nathalie began to scream at them in French. The bride's face, red with fury, provided all the translation Alice needed.

Chapter Twenty

There weren't many guests left in the big white marquee. Most of them, including Lara and Harry, had gone back to the ballroom where there was a DJ and dancing. Alice sat alone and sipped her espresso.

She was still feeling dazed, even though she was completely sober now. She knew what had happened over the past couple of hours, but it was all kind of blurry. Jack had made an announcement, something about a change of heart. His mother had become hysterical. When Monsieur de Trouville realized he could not recoup the expense, the event became a party. It was just like a wedding, but without a bride.

Jack came into the marquee, and took a seat beside her.

'What are you still doing in here?' he asked. 'Everyone's in the ballroom.'

'I just needed peace and quiet,' she told him.

'To savour your triumph?'

She smiled. 'How's your mother?' Alice asked.

'She'll recover. She's more upset about the fact that Nathalie absconded with the tiara.'

'Oh, no!'

Jack grinned. 'Don't worry. It was a fake. De Trouville is no fool. He wasn't about to lend out a prized possession.'

'How are *you* feeling?' she asked.

'Stupid,' he replied. 'And grateful. You saved my life, you know. I owe you.'

She didn't deny it. 'Just don't go making stupid mistakes with any more French girls. Or any other girls come to that.'

'No more mistakes,' he said quietly. He took her hand. Her heart was so full, she thought she would faint. But maybe that was because her stomach was so empty.

She looked at the remains of the croquembouche. 'I never got any of that.'

'Me neither,' Jack said. They got up and went over to the wedding cake. Jack found a plate and they piled the cream puffs on it.

'This is incredibly good,' Alice said.

'Yeah, it's almost worth almost getting married.' He

273

paused. 'You know, a couple of hours ago, for about a minute, I had a crazy idea. I thought maybe I *could* go through with the wedding ceremony. But with a different bride.'

Alice finished off the last cream puff and gazed longingly at the empty pedestal. 'That was lovely,' she said.

'Did you hear what I just said?' Jack asked.

Alice nodded. 'I'm too young to get married, Jack. And so are you.'

'Yeah, I suppose you're right,' he said. He put down the plate and took her in his arms.

'But when the time is right,' she whispered in his ear, 'I want the same cake.'

The
DUFF

Seventeen-year-old Bianca Piper
is smart, cynical, loyal - and well
aware that she's not the hot one
in her group of friends. But when
high-school jock and all round
moron Wesley Rush tells her she's
a DUFF - a Designated, Ugly Fat
Friend - Bianca does not see the
funny side.

She may not be a beauty but
she'd never stoop so low as to go
anywhere near the likes of Wesley
... Or would she? Bianca is about
to find out that attraction defies
looks and that sometimes your
sworn enemies can become your
best friends...

Funny, thoughtful and written by
the author when she was only
17, this novel will speak to every
teenage girl who has ever thought
they were a Duff.

April 2012

www.hodderchildrens.co.uk

Hodder
Children's
Books

SHUT OUT

A high school story of girls versus boys ... the battle is on!

The girls of Hamilton High School are going on strike. Sick of the rivalry between their boyfriends' American football and soccer teams, Lissa and her friends are determined that the boys won't see any action from them until they put an end to their immature pranks. But Lissa hasn't counted on a new sort of rivalry: an impossible girls-against-boys showdown that hinges on who will cave to their libidos first.

The new novel from the hugely popular author of *The DUFF*.

www.kodykeplinger.com
www.hodderchildrens.co.uk

Hodder Children's Books

EVERYTHING STARTS RIGHT HERE RIGHT NOW

MOMENTUM

SACI LLOYD

London, the near future. Energy wars are flaring across the globe - oil prices have gone crazy, regular power cuts are a daily occurrence. The cruel Kossak soldiers prowl the streets, keeping the Outsiders - the poor, the disenfranchised - in check. Hunter is a Citizen: one of the privileged of society, but with his passion for free running and his rebel friend Leo he cannot help but be fascinated by the Outsiders. So when he meets Outsider Uma, he is quickly drawn into their world - and into an electrifying and dangerous race to protect everything they hold dear.

A hugely exciting dystopian thriller from the immensely talented Costa-shortlisted author of The Carbon Diaries, Saci Lloyd.

'From its breathtaking opening ... an action-packed thriller with a warm heart' – The Guardian

Also available as an ebook

www.hodderchildrens.co.uk

Hodder Children's Books

When love is tangled up in magic, how do you know what's real?

Immerse yourself in the story of Anna, whose life changes for ever when she moves to the small town of Winter. In Winter she meets Seth Waters and unleashes a chain of events that leads them from love, to heartbreak, to mortal danger.

'This is not a fluffy romance tale; it's also an exciting story of a deadly power battle ... there's plenty in this debut for teenage readers who like romance, exciting battles and magic.'
The Telegraph

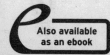

He's After Me

Chris Higgins

'His smile faded and our eyes held. A charge passed through me, like an electric shock.'

Anna meets Jem when her life is falling apart. He is everything Anna needs him to be. Her dad may have run off with a younger woman, her mum may be a wreck and her younger sister, Livi, is swerving off the rails - but as long as she has Jem, Anna will be OK.

And for the first time in her life Anna falls. Deeply and truly and intensely in love.

The end? Not quite...

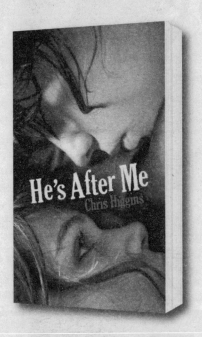

The Vampire of Highgate

Urban myth or real-life horror - what is the horrific truth behind one of London's darkest legends? Find out in a chilling new vampire saga ...

Kathy Bilic is adopted. Until now, she's had only a vague memory of her real family. But disturbing dreams of her sister Amber have begun to wake her in the night. When Kathy hits London to find her sister, the murderous trail she uncovers reveals the full nightmare of her heritage. Her sister's fate is in the hands of the Vampire of Highgate.

Gripping, atmospheric and sexy, this is British horror at its best.

www.hodderchildrens.co.uk

Hodder Children's Books

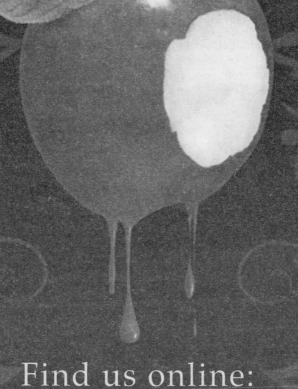